Forever

F-WORD
BOOK FOUR

E. DAVIES

Forever / E. Davies. – 1st ed.
ISBN: 978-1-912245-22-2

Forever

CHAPTER
One

JAKE

"ONE MORE THING BEFORE YOU GO: HAVE YOU CONSIDERED your fertility lately?"

"Uhhh." Jake ran a hand through his hair, looking around the whitewashed office to avoid Dr. Lume's gaze. His stomach gave an unpleasant jolt at the subject. The past six years had trained him out of thinking about pregnancy in general.

He'd had other priorities, to say the least. He hadn't expected the subject to come up during his yearly checkup, but then, he'd been avoiding it for long enough.

"I haven't been lying awake thinking about it. Why?"

"Okay." Dr. Lume drummed her fingers on the keyboard, then turned to face him. "It might be time to devote some thought to it, Jake."

Jake nodded. "You're right," he agreed. He knew as well as anyone what the official guidance said. Three to five years of hormone treatment meant a hysterectomy, though nothing definitive about the risks of skipping one had been found. "I just wasn't ready to think about it until now."

"It's important," Dr. Lume told him. "It might be safe to forgo, and it might not be. We can't say for sure that either option is safe, but I want to make you aware of the choice. The benefits are obvious. We might be able to lower your dose slightly. You've been on testosterone for...?" She glanced at the computer for her notes.

"Five and a half years," Jake said absently. He was used to answering the basics without even thinking.

"That's right. I can't believe it's been so long already." She gave him a warm smile, and he relaxed.

"Yeah. Time flies." Jake had had a lot in his life to make the time go quickly, but not a stable living environment or another guy with factory-default plumbing, with whom he could or wanted to make babies.

At least, not a steady guy. He'd met enough one-night stands that could be sperm donor material, but co-parenting?

No. He'd have to know someone really well to share parenting duties. That was a *we've been dating for a couple years and we just saw a cute baby* kind of talk.

"When we discussed this a few years ago, you said you were potentially interested in having children," she pressed gently.

Jake nodded. "Yeah. I've always wanted one or two of my own." Sure, he could try egg storage and surrogacy and all that stuff, but that was incredibly expensive and meant getting someone else involved.

Many trans guys would have been dysphoric about the idea of pregnancy, but Jake didn't resent his internal equipment. It was out of sight, out of mind for him. Even thinking about going off testosterone for a year or longer wasn't awful now that he was read as male consistently. He'd been himself for so long that he could almost start to forget his old life.

Except for one thing: he'd always wanted kids when he was grown up. It had never occurred to him that he *was* a grownup now.

Fuck, that was terrifying. Who had given him the keys to adulthood?

"You also know that we don't know the long-term effects of testosterone. If I remember right, gamete storage was too expensive for you to consider back then… but now?"

"It still would be," Jake said and shook his head. "And you're right. I've just been caught up in my own little world for the last couple years." Living on the outskirts of L.A., cobbling together work as a production assistant on different shows and at restaurants, had kept him busy.

"I know surgery recovery was hard on you last time," Dr. Lume said.

Jake snorted and nodded. "Understatement." The stress and recovery from top surgery had been hard to deal with, especially in his career.

She nodded. "So take your time and think about how you feel about another surgery—there are risks to both choices. There could be long-term complications associated with keeping those parts, but surgery is always serious. I've talked to you about those risks before."

"Yeah," Jake said quietly. Some men had died from the complications of hysterectomies. The risks were real.

But now wasn't really the best time to get pregnant. He couldn't very well wait tables or run around sets with a huge belly, could he? He wasn't quiet about his trans status, and he was lucky to live in a state where he could afford to be so open about it. At least he had the law on his side in California, and he probably wasn't going to end up unemployed and homeless.

The practicality he'd had to develop over the last six years of independence kicked in.

"I don't know if it's in the cards for me," Jake said quietly. "I don't have a boyfriend. Can't seem to get one around here who wants more than a hot fling, you know? Not that that's not great, but… not for babies."

"Whether you want to try co-parenting or single parenting, there are all kinds of options." She tapped her fingers on the desk and thought for a moment before lighting up. "I know. I'll give you a business card. Plus is an HIV charity specifically for the queer community, with a trans-inclusive mission. I went to a talk by someone there. They've told me that they're well-connected to other organizations and resources. So if you want guidance or peer support, they could probably help you find queer family and parenting groups."

The offer of connections—of community—meant a lot to Jake. "That would be great."

Dr. Lume smiled at him and leaned in. "You've never let things stand in the way of what *you* want before. So think about what that is, and then we'll work on getting you there. Okay?"

Not for the first time, Jake thanked all his lucky stars that he had a doctor like Dr. Lume on his side. Her compassion and willingness to research what she didn't know had been a lifeline for him numerous times throughout the last six years. He cleared his throat gruffly and scratched the stubble on his jawline. "Thanks," he said, trying to sum up everything into the one word as he rose to his feet.

She heard what he really meant, judging by her smile back. "You're welcome. Take care."

The office door closed behind him and Jake escaped to the smoggy L.A. air. He was alone with his thoughts again, the first and loudest of which was, *At the end of the day, it's just me.*

It had been that way for the last six years, since his parents had told him not to come home until he'd changed his mind about "fitting in with trends," as they put it.

While Jake was at it, he'd left not just his childhood home and family, but the whole state. Running away to L.A. had always been his dream. What better time to chase it?

God, he'd been a crazy kid, but somehow, it had all worked out. Jake had landed a series of jobs as a waitress at first, and then as a waiter. Planned Parenthood here had saved his fucking life when he'd started testosterone six months after moving here.

His lost tips from roleplaying a bubbly girl were more than compensated by the tips for being his real self, and even if they hadn't been, he'd do it again in a heartbeat. His smile was rarely forced now, and it didn't feel like his self-esteem was being ground into the dust by every *she* obnoxiously thrown at him by a table who'd clocked him.

On set, he'd gotten respect almost immediately from most of the people he worked with. He hadn't stopped getting calls to work on set, which had been a real fear. Now, he was less passionate about keeping Hollywood's wheels greased, but it was still an interesting and rewarding string of occasional gigs to help keep the lights on.

Jake chewed his nail as he pulled out of the clinic parking lot, driving automatically towards the grocery store. He went through his usual shopping without thinking twice, too.

His attention was devoted to looking twice at every kid in the store, imagining what it would be like if one of them were *his*.

Sure, it was terrifying as hell to have to give directions to a tiny person whose hell-bent aim seemed to be destroying themselves and everything around them, but...

There was something that tugged at his heartstrings deep down. His desire for kids hadn't changed since realizing he was trans, or since transitioning. It was deep-seated, and it came from a different part of him. When he'd found out that transitioning and parenting weren't either/or options, he'd been overjoyed.

Dr. Lume was right. Worrying about who the sperm donor was could come later. He had to get over himself. If he waited until romance found him, he was putting his life in the hands of fate, and he'd done that enough for one lifetime.

So it was time for Jake to start building the kind of life where he could support a kid. He just had no idea what that kind of life would even look like.

CHAPTER

Two

TRISTAN

"W‍HO THE HELL NOMINATED ME AS THE UMPIRE?" T‍RISTAN dashed out of the way, squirming between two desks as he held his hands up to show he was not getting involved.

River and Zeph were on a collision course. Each straddled an office chair backwards, holding a rolled-up poster under their armpit. They were both making horse noises as they propelled themselves across the office floor as fast as they could.

Denver poked his head out of his office and snorted. "Just another lunch hour at Plus. You get used to it around here," he told Tristan. "At least they're not playing tonsil hockey."

"Yet!" Zeph crowed. He knocked River's poster askew and sent his boyfriend toppling off the chair. "Loser gives a blowjob in the bathroom later."

Kyle, River's best friend and the only one of them besides Denver who actually *worked* here, was laughing his ass off. "Victory to Zeph!"

"Sanitize the bathroom when you're done," Denver advised them with a mild smile. He ducked back into his office, no doubt to continue the endless stream of paperwork he seemed to handle. Nothing seemed to faze him.

Tristan covered his face and laughed. He had to admit, this beat sitting around by himself in the parking lot to drop off Zeph to see his boyfriend here, hiding his face in case anyone saw him. Drawbacks of being an up-and-coming and very closeted actor.

Zeph had eventually talked him around with promises of donuts in the office. Even Tristan could take a diet cheat day for really good donuts.

"Your turn," River started to say before the entryphone rang.

Kyle cleared his throat and glanced guiltily around, sweeping the posters to the side and answering. "This is Plus." Then he paused and nodded. "Of course! I'll be right down for a chat."

Tristan had heard that they got a fair number of walk-ins looking for information, advice, or referrals. Plus was one of the foremost HIV education and activism charities, and they'd made a name for themselves in the gay community. They had made a point of being trans-inclusive and of supporting PrEP—both attention-grabbing stances.

"No, no, stay here," Kyle urged the gang when Zeph started to stand up. "I think we have a few more rounds left. And then the spoils of victory to claim."

Tristan blushed and shook his head, looking around at the office. Most of the other employees had gone out for lunch nearby. Denver's boyfriend, Sam, ran a little diner that had become their informal gathering spot.

Kyle was here, though, which meant River was here to keep him company, and Zeph was devoted to River. It was sweet to see—Tristan didn't have many close friends, so seeing Zeph truly happy meant a lot to him... even if it did make white-hot jealousy prickle deep in his gut.

Jealousy was an embarrassing emotion at the best of times. Feeling it about his best friend, who of all people, deserved to be happy? Tristan felt bad. And that only led to a self-defeating cycle of feeling bad about feeling bad.

"I figured after this, we could head to the gym for practice," Zeph offered. "We haven't sparred in a while."

Fighting a former MMA fighter was most people's idea of a bad time, but Tristan had known—and sparred against—Zeph for long enough to trust him. He only did it when he was pretty sure he wasn't about to get a call-back, and Zeph usually tried to avoid major bruises.

It was a great way to burn energy, but all the sexual tension in this damn office had Tristan considering other ways... a situation that was not aided by the sight of the man who followed Kyle through the doors just a minute later.

He'd flirted with—or avoided flirting with—enough guys in this town that faces blurred together, but he distinctly remembered this one.

Tristan considered the classic question first: *Have we slept together?*

The guy's name—Jake—and where they'd met clicked in his mind at the exact same moment that Jake saw him.

"Oh, shit." Tristan laughed awkwardly. "Hi."

"Hey." Jake tipped his chin up with a bright smile. He'd only gotten hotter since he'd worked on the little indie film Tristan had taken on during a slow period in bookings.

Tristan couldn't forget the man whose job it had been to pour water bottles down his shirt one hot summer week. Thank god the water had been cold—and blissful relief in the summer heat—because he'd been dangerously close to popping a boner every time he made eye contact with Jake.

Jake had grown out his stubble into almost leading-man looks of his own, though Tristan sensed that his bubbly personality would shut down in front of a camera. A lot of people who were the most vibrant behind the scenes were like that, while many actors were actually shy when the cameras were off.

"How's it going?" Jake added awkwardly, glancing to Zeph and then River. He snuck another peek under those long lashes at Tristan.

Tristan's cheeks were hot. "Good. You? Been getting a lot of work?" *Smooth, get to the topic you wanna avoid right away.* He fidgeted and cleared his throat. "I'm not… I haven't, uh…"

"Yeah. Don't worry, your secret's safe," Jake told him simply, crossing his heart in a little X.

God, he was adorable.

Tristan could feel the others staring at him as he blushed. It was going to become a perpetual cycle of blushing harder and being more awkward if he wasn't careful. "Cool. Hey, you wanted my workout routine back then, right?" It had only been two years ago, and he remembered chatting about workouts back then.

Jake's brows shot up. "You remembered."

"Y-Yeah," Tristan shrugged and smiled. "Not a lot else to do between takes that day, was there? Anyway, this guy creates most of my routines," he jerked his thumb at Zeph. "Zeph, Jake. He worked on the same set as me."

"I gathered," Zeph said. Tristan could tell it was taking a hell of a lot of self-control not to tease him then and there. He could have kissed his best friend—not that River would have let him—for the sudden and uncharacteristic discretion.

"I'll just go get you the phone number," Kyle murmured and trotted to his office, casting them one more curious glance over his shoulder. With one fewer person to diffuse the energy here, the tension thickened between Tristan and Jake. He could feel it, and he could feel Zeph and River noticing it, but there wasn't a damn thing he could do about it.

"So, uh, Zeph was an MMA fighter," Tristan forged onward, trying not to let his gaze linger on those full lips and gorgeous, bright eyes. "We spar sometimes at gyms and stuff."

"Oh, that's cool." Jake smiled at Zeph, and for half a weird second, Tristan was... *jealous* of him.

Jesus. Here he was, jealous of his best friend, who was happily partnered up with the man who was actually leaning into him that very moment. For being smiled at by a guy who'd once poured water down his shirt.

Tristan had often said he didn't believe in such a thing as chemistry, because all of it was replicable. Actors made the choice to create chemistry or not. But this? This was something else. And all of a sudden, he was desperate not to let Jake walk out that door without his number.

"If you're interested, I can show you more stuff Zeph's taught me, or you can like. Go out. With us. To the gym."

Not Tristan's smoothest pickup line, but it worked. "Sure! That'd be awesome," Jake admitted. "It gets hard motivating yourself sometimes."

"Oh, I know how that is." Tristan looked over at Zeph. "He kicks my ass a lot, when I need it. And vice versa."

"That's what friends are for," Zeph said cheerily. "You

guys swap numbers and let me know if you need ass-kicking or a routine. I literally design routines for fun."

"He's not lying," Tristan grinned, awkwardly holding out his phone. "Wanna… swap numbers?"

"Yeah!" Jake fumbled to grab his own phone and dropped it, then cursed under his breath and scooped it up, checking the screen for damage before handing it over. "God. Sorry. Here."

Tristan stifled his amusement. At least he wasn't the only one making an idiot out of himself. Small consolation when he was going to get teased for years to come about this, but consolation nonetheless.

"Here you are." Kyle came back with a sheet of folded paper just as they exchanged phones again.

Jake smiled again. "Thanks. Sorry to drop in unannounced."

"Oh, we always welcome drop-ins," Denver spoke up from the office behind them, making them both jump. He waved slightly and grinned. "Especially when they have such fabulous hair. Where *do* you get it done, darling?"

Tristan tuned out the conversation for a minute just to watch Jake's lips move before realizing how pervy that was. *But I can't keep my eyes off him*, he thought.

Jake waved and headed out after a minute. "See you later," he said to them all, but it was clear it was aimed at Tristan.

Tristan just waved back. He couldn't untie his tongue long enough to wish him a nice day or anything.

The minute Jake was gone, all four men—Denver, Kyle, River, and Zeph—stared at him.

"What?" Tristan snorted. He tried his hardest to play dumb.

"You're finally getting laid with a guy who isn't further in the closet than Narnia," Zeph commented and held out a hand for a high-five.

Tristan scoffed, but there was no point in denying his intentions. "Yeah, whatever. We'll see."

"Oh, he was into you," River seconded with a grin. "We know fuck-me eyes when we see them."

"Mmhmm." Kyle folded his arms and pursed his lips. "Don't deny it."

"I've felt less chemistry in Hallmark movies." Denver winked when Tristan glared at them all.

Still, Tristan's cheeks were flushed with pleasure. These guys all knew each other's secrets, and that kind of community was incredible to feel. Maybe being out had its perks. Meeting other gay men, not afraid of the consequences, was an amazing feeling.

It couldn't be worse than a soulless Grindr hookup, all the while hoping the wrong person didn't out him at the wrong moment. At least getting together with Jake, who had already promised that his secret was safe, might be fun.

He had nothing to lose by going for it, right?

CHAPTER

Three

JAKE

LIFE WAS FUCKED UP IN THE BEST POSSIBLE WAY.

Going to an HIV charity to get help finding a queer family support group was strange enough. He hadn't expected to meet a group of such colorful and friendly guys there. And one of them being Tristan?

He'd walked out with contact details for a guy who was starting a co-parenting group and would talk to him, a website for a local trans-positive doula, details of a trans men's support group… and Tristan Bailey's phone number.

Of course he remembered Tristan, and that one week on set. He'd been trying his hardest to stay professional while Tristan cast him fleeting but unmistakable glances, like he'd like to rub their sweating bodies together in a private spot somewhere.

He'd been a couple years on T at that point and being gendered correctly most of the time. Having the lead actor himself pay him attention had been a ridiculous confidence boost.

Jake had rubbed one out more than once to the memories

of being close enough to Tristan to almost taste his sweat. And it looked like the feeling was mutual.

He could die happy now.

Jake giggled to himself when he got a text—an actual *text!*—minutes after he got home. Tristan wasn't wasting time, and he appreciated that.

He wasn't a fame-chaser. He counted exactly zero actors in his little black book—that he knew about, anyway. Everyone here seemed to want a turn in front of the camera.

But something about Tristan's physical presence had drawn him in from the first moment. Maybe the hint of conflict he'd seen every time Tristan had looked at him. Because of it, he'd never made a move, and he'd regretted it since then.

He'd always suspected that "it's not you, it's me" was at work. Tristan was deep in the closet, judging by his Google search results. Which was why it was such a surprise to find him just casually hanging out at Plus. This wasn't an attempt to buy his silence, was it? He made a mental note to confirm that before he got down to cock-sucking business.

The text was simple.

Zeph had to bail. Wanna see me at the gym?

He couldn't answer fast enough.

Sure!

Then Tristan texted the address, and Jake was sprinting into the house to change into workout clothes.

Since he and Dr. Lume had decided to stop his testosterone, his hormones had been all over the place. Even if this wasn't some irresistible biological impulse, he kind of hoped getting laid would help calm his libido down. He hadn't expected that to get stronger after stopping hormones—quite the opposite.

He was on a late shift at the restaurant, and he was gonna hate himself tomorrow for hitting the gym *before* work, but he didn't care. If this was his "in" with Tristan, he was gonna take it.

Hopefully his in-and-out. For all he wanted a future, he wasn't against having fun now, either. Sometimes, chemistry couldn't be ignored. They'd already lost touch once after that week of barely-veiled sexual tension.

It would just be fucking tragic to ignore that pull twice.

"Pull—come on. *That's* it!" Tristan grinned as he hauled Jake to his feet. "See? Your arm is stable this way. If you let it rotate, you can fuck up your body for life."

Jake was a hell of a lot more worried about getting fucked tonight, but he did all he could to remember Tristan's tutorial. "You might have to remind me next week," he laughed. "I'm easily distracted."

Tristan's eyes sparkled with amusement. They were alone in the corner of the gym—a quiet, industrial place, not the kind of flashy one Jake had somehow imagined he'd go to. "By what?"

There it was—the invitation to dance.

Jake took it. "By good-looking guys hauling me around," he answered, letting his gaze flicker up and down Tristan's body. "Especially when they're shirtless and *right there.*"

Tristan's body was hot as fuck, and resisting the urge to nibble it—even just a little—had taken eighty percent of his willpower over the last half-hour.

"Mmm. I could take this workout somewhere else, if you

wanted to," Tristan suggested, his voice low. "Hit the showers?"

"I don't usually shower in gyms." Jake wasn't sure how much Tristan had heard about him while he was on set, or how much he remembered. He swallowed hard, following Tristan at a leisurely stroll toward the shower. "I tend to surprise guys."

"With your incredibly sexy body?" Tristan inquired, winking.

Jake only realized it was a gentle joke to defuse the situation after he'd already started correcting him. "With my scars, and the dick situation. I don't know if you remember…"

Tristan touched his shoulder. "I remember you being pretty open about it on set. How about showering with just me, then?"

"You're fine with it?"

Tristan gave him a warm smile. "I'm hitting on you, aren't I? We'll figure out something that works for us both. It's no big deal."

"Okay. Awesome." Jake grinned with relief. He didn't usually get too worked up about whether any one guy was gonna be an ass, because there was always another dick attached to a nicer guy out there.

But this time? He wanted this dick, *and* this guy. Now that the possibility of rejection was gone, he was nearly dizzy with relief.

The chemistry between them was exactly as strong as it had been a minute ago, and Tristan hadn't fallen into *ask Jake a million questions about his genitals and then compliment his bravery for being alive* mode. That was always such a goddamn turn-off. Nobody wanted to feel like a high school sex ed teacher right before hooking up.

"We could head for my place," Tristan suggested. "If you wanna shower at mine, then we'll have a lot more privacy. And a king-sized bed." He winked.

Jake licked his lips. "Fuck, yeah."

Tristan cast him a quick sideways glance, then said quietly, "A friend of a friend is… stealth, I think you'd call it? I forget. But I know a little bit."

"Oh." Jake couldn't help but wonder if it was an actor. If gay actors had to hide themselves in Hollywood, he had no doubt trans actors did, too. "Oh, cool."

Tristan grinned at him. "And I've wanted you since we shot that movie."

He thought about me? Jake blushed down to his toes and Tristan chuckled warmly. "Me, too," Jake admitted. "I was gonna pick you up, but you always looked so uncertain, you know?"

They were alone in the locker room as they swapped sweaty t-shirts for fresh ones, and Jake turned away from the wall to let Tristan see the faded scars along his chest. Once red, they were now pale and less attention-catching.

"Nice pecs," Tristan complimented him with a smirk. "But yeah. I *was* uncertain back then."

"So was I." Jake hadn't quite hit his slutty stage that summer. He'd still been reeling from life: top surgery, then recovery, and then scrambling to get a new job before he worked himself even further into debt. Debt was a hell of a libido-squasher.

They could barely keep their hands off each other on the way to the parking lot. Tristan kept touching his arm and wrist, and it was all Jake could do not to push him up against the car and kiss him.

Not here. Not in public, even if it's deserted. It was weird being around someone with something so big to hide, but Jake completely understood Tristan's reasons.

"Wanna follow me? Or leave your car here? It's up to you," Tristan offered.

Jake licked his lips. "Better follow you."

"Better not lose me," Tristan winked and headed to his car with a cheeky wave.

"Oh, I wouldn't." Jake gazed after Tristan for a few moments before remembering to actually open his own car door. "Not a chance," he murmured under his breath.

CHAPTER

Four

TRISTAN

It wasn't the first time he'd invited a hookup over to his place instead of sneaking out and grabbing a cheap hotel. Hell, it wasn't even the first time he'd picked up a guy from that very gym.

So why the hell was Tristan so nervous about the state of his place now that Jake was following him home?

Even though he'd been in far worse places to meet guys, Tristan hadn't tidied up in a few days, and he found himself weirdly worried about whether Jake would think he was a slob.

Sex. That's all this is, he reminded himself. *You don't even know the guy. Jesus. Just because you see your friends off getting hitched... some very publicly, with Instagram sponsors and every-thing... doesn't mean that you get to have that life.*

That was Tristan's damage—his choice he'd made so he could live the career of his dreams. This wasn't exactly the career of his dreams, but he wasn't going to let his resent-ment bleed into the rest of his life.

He was just going to enjoy reconnecting with the one

who'd got away, preferably with full-body contact and plenty of tongue.

It wasn't the first time Tristan had met a trans guy. He'd known a few, but he hadn't slept with any of them, that he knew of. But then again, he tried to hook up as little as possible to satisfy his urges, to minimize the risk of being outed.

From what he remembered on set, Jake was admirably open about his own body and life, but as for Tristan? No way. Tristan didn't want the world knowing anything that was none of their business.

Once Kyle's boyfriend, Nic, had gotten to know Tristan enough through their little network of friends to trust him, he'd told him that he was trans and stealth. As far as Nic was concerned, "don't make it a big deal" was the rule to live by, so Tristan reminded himself of that as he parked outside his apartment building.

It wasn't as fancy as most people would expect from a B-list actor, but that helped him avoid attention. Some of his friends were well-versed in the art of sneaking around in plain sight, but Tristan couldn't guiltily avoid eye contact with a concierge on a regular basis.

"You didn't lose me," Tristan commented.

Jake locked his car door and grinned. "What did I tell you? I really need that shower."

Tristan laughed. Now that he was on his home turf, he wasn't afraid to slide an arm around Jake's waist. He leaned in to playfully sniff. His lips touched Jake's neck as he did so, brushing and dragging gently across the sensitive skin. "Nope. Smells fine to me."

Salty, sweaty, and full of delicious pheromones or something that made him want to pin him to the side of the building and take his time peeling their clothes off. How long had it been since he'd gotten laid, anyway? Obviously too long.

"Okay, you'd better show me your place pronto," Jake murmured, his breath quick and sharp.

Tristan couldn't stop himself, now that they were so close together. The attraction building under his skin was making his thoughts run wild with the desire to do more—to spread soap along this man's body and explore an inch at a time.

Oops. He was getting hard, and walking was about to become awkward as fuck. "Agreed. This way."

They made it to the elevator before making out, which Tristan considered an impressive act of self-restraint.

Their lips slid together in a slow, warm promise of what was to come. Jake tasted like mint—he must have snuck one while he was in the car. Damn, that was a good taste on him.

Before he could tell Jake so, Tristan found himself spinning around, back against the elevator wall as Jake kissed him hard.

Fuck, that was hot. Jake kissed him like he wanted to screw him through the wall, and Tristan's knees responded to that by almost giving way.

"First door on the right," he managed when the elevator doors opened.

Jake kissed him once more before dragging him out through the doors by the hand.

Tristan fumbled to get the door opened, and closed again, before Jake grabbed him by the cheeks and kissed him with all the luxury of privacy.

"You *do* live alone?" Jake pulled back and eyed Tristan for a moment.

Tristan laughed. "Yeah. Good question. Yeah, I do." He

could barely remember his name right now, but he was at least sure that he didn't have a roommate. Probably.

God, it was hard to focus when Jake was giving him the fuck-me eyes. No, no roommate. Next order of business…

"Shower?" Jake suggested, the tone more demanding than suggestive.

"Shower," Tristan nodded. He was hard as anything already, and it took him a second to decide where he wanted to begin stripping off. "Bathroom's, uh, through there."

His place was nice enough—an open layout with sliding doors separating the spacious master bedroom from the rest of the place. Best of all, an en suite… with a shower and a tub.

"Shit, this is nice." Jake raised an eyebrow and looked over at Tristan.

Tristan grinned sheepishly and shrugged. How different things looked through the eyes of someone who wasn't neck-deep in Hollywood's "keeping up with the Joneses" disorder.

"You could throw great parties here," Jake commented.

"I try not to, so they don't try to raise the rent on me and squeeze me out." Tristan grinned.

"Only medium parties?"

"Very reasonable parties," Tristan agreed, grinning. He wrapped his arms around Jake's waist and kissed him, walking him backward to the bedroom. Though Jake tensed up, his breathing harsh between kisses, he let Tristan guide him.

There was already a spark of trust, then. That made for better sex. Tristan grinned, and then Jake nipped his lower lip. "Oof!"

"No laughing at me."

"I'm not laughing. I'm…" Tristan trailed off for a moment as he realized it at the same pace as he said it. "I'm happy."

"It's been that long, huh?" Jake winked.

Tristan shook his head. "No. Yes. I don't know, I can't think straight," he admitted. "I just like the chemistry. It feels good."

Jake looked startled for a moment, and then he lowered his eyes, his cheeks flushing pink. Oh, man. That was adorable as hell. "Cool. Me too."

"Shower's through here." Tristan wouldn't embarrass him by pointing out that he was blushing. Jake was probably already aware. He started stripping first, hoping to make Jake more comfortable. "Are you fine with seeing me naked?"

"I won't lie, I was hoping to." Jake threw him a wink, seemingly back on his game now. "Showering would be awkward otherwise. So would fucking."

Tristan grinned as he stepped out of his underwear, which left him naked and half-hard already. "I like the way you think."

That was an understatement—Jake made him want to peel every layer of clothing off, fuck him hard, and then hold him and listen to him talk for hours.

Tristan mentally kicked himself a moment after he thought it. God, he couldn't just go thinking things like that based on half-remembered conversations, longing glances, and one sexual tension-laden workout.

Clearly, he needed something else in his life. He couldn't find it all in one man. That way lay disappointment.

"Then you'll love the way I suck you," Jake answered with a smirk and an appreciative glance down at Tristan's cock. He peeled off his t-shirt.

"I can't wait." Tristan's eyes lingered for a moment on the

scars. Then, Tristan glanced down, letting his gaze rove over Jake's body from head to toe.

Jake's shoulders rose in a slightly defensive way as he dropped his jeans. Interesting, and oddly enough, it made Tristan want to compliment him even more.

"Oh, hello." Jake's bulge drew Tristan's gaze.

Jake laughed. "We don't get the choice of growing or showing when we pack. It's all showing."

He beckoned Tristan closer, and Tristan stepped forward, letting his hands run up Jake's chest from his waistband first. He traced the scar around one nipple and cast a concerned look up at him.

"Oh, I only have partial feeling there. I lost a lot of feeling, but... worth it." Jake shrugged it off like no big deal. Even though Tristan was kind of in awe of his fortitude, he'd respect Jake's clear wish not to linger on it.

Tristan leaned down, catching the other nipple in his mouth. Whether or not Jake felt it, Tristan wanted him to see how hot it was, visually... and wanted to test how Jake responded.

Jake chuckled, and then he laced his fingers in Tristan's hair. He pulled him closer, pressing his chest into Tristan's mouth.

That dominant streak was hot as hell.

Jake guided his mouth to the other nipple, and then let go of his head, so Tristan eagerly kissed up his chest to his neck.

"You have gorgeous lips," Jake told him.

Tristan beamed. Jake was hitting buttons Tristan hadn't even known he had. The way he took over and effortlessly maneuvered Tristan around, like he already knew what he wanted...

"What do you want me to do?" Tristan murmured, taking a chance.

It worked. Jake straightened up as he ran his hand slowly down Tristan's arm, then to the small of his back. "Turn the shower on and give me a show."

Tristan almost slipped in his eagerness to do so. He grabbed the shower stall for balance, then leaned in and turned on the hot water.

Oh, fuck. Jake was stripping now, and it was the hottest thing Tristan had seen. He peeled his underwear off slowly, revealing a jock strap underneath and what looked like a silicone cock. It was realistic enough for the big screen, with blue-tinted veins and a gorgeous head.

Tristan licked his lips as he stepped into the shower, rubbing the water across his own chest and down to his own hard cock. He stroked it a few times, making eye contact with Jake as he straightened up.

"You like that?" Jake grinned. "Because, baby, I can be as big as you want, and stay hard as long as you want."

Tristan hadn't even thought about that before. He grinned back at Jake, his body tingling with anticipation as the words sank in. "Are you more of a top?"

For some reason, he hadn't expected that. Which was dumb when he thought about it—he didn't expect any cis guys he slept with to automatically be tops or bottoms, whether they were super-femme or muscled powerhouses. A lot of guys did judge by looks, but Tristan tried not to.

Jake half-smiled as he watched Tristan. "Yeah, sometimes. But I like bottoming, too. Anal or frontal sex. I'm just a slut for someone's dick going somewhere good. I guess that makes me vers."

"Frontal..." Tristan started to ask before he figured it out.

His cheeks flushed. Again with the stupid preconceptions—he'd just kind of assumed Jake wouldn't use that hole. But why the hell not? Many of the gay men he knew would use whatever was available, as long as it felt good. "Ah."

Jake snorted with amusement and wiggled out of his jock strap.

The cock that had been nestled underneath the silicone was pink and clearly hard under the foreskin. Sure, it was small, but the way Jake looked, talked, even smelled—Tristan didn't care about size.

There was so much more to Jake than a couple inches of skin.

Tristan ached with need for him. He beckoned to Jake, turning sideways to indicate that he was leaving room for him in the shower stall.

"You're hard," Tristan whispered when Jake reached him. He ran a hand down Jake's hip, his thumb brushing the indent around his hipbone. "I can tell."

Jake's body twitched, his breath catching in his throat. "Surprised you can tell?"

"I didn't know what to expect," Tristan admitted. "I don't think I've ever seen a trans guy naked. In real life or porn."

"There's porn out there with us," Jake smiled. "We can watch it sometime if you want."

Tristan nodded, letting his hands rest on Jake's hips. "You'll have to tell me what to do here."

He'd slept with women twice and regretted it, but this was nothing like those experiences. The energy between him and Jake was like the other guys he'd slept with so far, but Tristan didn't know how to please him the same way.

He could deep-throat like a pro, but how did he suck Jake's cock without relying on deep-throating to impress him? What if Jake hated it? What if he couldn't make Jake come?

"You're fine," Jake assured him with a grin, running his hand up Tristan's chest. "Just do what comes naturally. I'm used to being an experiment."

The words cut Tristan to the bone. For half a second, he felt guilty, and then angry. "You're not—you're not just an experiment."

"No. I'm a prize-winning project," Jake joked, running his hand down Tristan's chest and wrapping it lightly around his shaft. "First in science fair, two years running."

Taken aback yet again by this man, Tristan laughed. He'd expected a tender moment of... well, fragile self-esteem. Like Tristan himself had felt when *he* was someone's experiment.

But Jake seemed to be more resilient than him, and certainly more graceful about keeping the mood up.

I've really gotta stop trying to guess what to expect, he thought. *Every time I do, Jake shoots me down... and rightly so.*

Tristan wanted him even more badly now. Jake seemed to radiate the confidence that Tristan did on-screen, but off-screen? In bed? Yeah, right. Tristan faked it, and he never quite made it.

Jake carefully stepped closer, until their cocks touched. As he ground against Tristan, the hot shower water streaming down their bodies helped them slide together. The small, hard nub pressing against Tristan's shaft ignited electric-hot need deep in his belly.

"Yes," Tristan gasped, his nails digging into Jake's hips. "Does that feel good, too?"

"Yes. It's the same as the head of your cock," Jake told him simply, kissing his neck. "Just, most of mine is inside my body."

Tristan blinked a few times, trying to go back to high school biology in his head. He couldn't remember ever having heard that. "Really?"

Jake sighed. "Oh, the American education system. Speaking of boner-killing subjects."

"Sorry," Tristan laughed. He rolled his head back to let Jake kiss his throat instead, thrusting his hips forward. "Pass me the bodywash?"

"Oh, yeah." Jake handed over the bottle.

Tristan poured the cool liquid into his hands. He spread it across Jake's back, keeping their bodies pressed together for now as he ran his hands over Jake's shoulders and shoulder blades. He traced them slowly down each side of his spine, taking the time to feel every indent of his ribs and line of his muscles.

By the time he got to Jake's lower back, Jake was squirming against him, wrapping his arms around Tristan's back.

God, he had a nice ass. Tristan marveled over it as he let slick hands run down over it, then across the furry backs of his thighs, as far down as he could reach, and up the front of his body.

Jake peeled himself away from Tristan, leaving Tristan dripping wet and achingly hard. He leaned back against the wall, spreading his legs. The sultry gaze he cast Tristan left him in no doubt as to what he was supposed to do now.

Tristan ran his hands up the inside of Jake's thighs, smiling at the way the hot water left ripples in the hair across his skin. As his fingertips dragged toward Jake's cock, Jake held his breath, his knees visibly shaking. God, he was sensitive, and Tristan intended to take full advantage of that.

He parted his hands to trace Jake's hips and run up toward his chest instead.

"Fuck," Jake hissed, pouting at him.

Tristan grinned. "Patience, sexy."

"Says the man who couldn't wait to get me in the shower."

"But now I have you here," Tristan growled, leaning in to press slow kisses across Jake's shoulder and neck. The sharp scent of mint from his body wash assaulted his nose, but it was sweeter for being spread across Jake's skin. "And I want to tease you until you're desperate for me."

Jake moaned breathlessly and pushed forward, but Tristan kept his hips angled so that his aching shaft didn't grind against him. Teasing Jake until he begged was going to be so much fun.

"Fine," Jake mumbled, scooping the bottle of body wash up and filling a palm with the liquid. He spread it across Tristan's chest and stomach in quick circles, his jaw set in a defiant expression.

God, Tristan responded well to that. His touches slowed as if he were subconsciously waiting for Jake's orders.

Jake grinned, lifting his chin as he stared at Tristan. "Turn around."

Tristan nearly slipped in his rush to do so, but Jake grabbed him by the elbow. Still, Tristan's heart pounded from the adrenaline rush, and from the need that had been thrumming through his veins for hours.

"Careful," Jake murmured and pushed him up against the wall. "You don't want to end up in the ER before I fuck you."

"Are you implying I might end up there after you do?" Tristan exclaimed, unable to help his laugh as he turned to look at Jake, spreading his hands against the wall. Jake was fun as well as funny, and it made him even sexier.

"Depends how much of a size queen you are." Jake winked and pressed up behind him, his cock nestling between the cheeks of Tristan's ass. He wasn't big enough to slide inside, but Tristan could feel it against the sensitive nerve endings around his hole.

Suddenly, he had a damn good idea what it would be like to be pinned here and filled up with Jake's cock—whatever size cock he wanted.

Tristan whimpered, his nails scrabbling for grip against the tiles of his shower wall. He bowed his head, pressing the top of his head against the wall as he stared down at himself. God, he was hard. When he slid his hand down the wall toward his cock, Jake grabbed his wrist and pulled it back up the wall again.

"Oh," Tristan whispered, twisting to look at Jake again.

Jake met his gaze and leaned in for a gentle kiss. "I want to be rough with you." He rested his chin on Tristan's shoulder, and his stubble scraped across the sensitive skin. "You okay with that?"

"Please," Tristan whispered. He couldn't compose his thoughts any better than that, but his body throbbed in pleasure. The itch that Jake was scratching was so deeply buried that he hadn't even thought about it that much.

But he sure as hell knew he wanted Jake inside him, over him, and all around him.

"Show me your bedroom." Jake shut off the water and stepped out, grabbing a fluffy towel from the shelf nearby. He wrapped it around Tristan's shoulders and used it to tug him toward him for another kiss.

"Oooh. Yes, sir," Tristan said and grinned. It was awkward for Tristan to walk with his boner in this kind of state, but he didn't want to waste a moment. He toweled himself off fast, watching Jake do the same.

Jake wrapped his towel around his waist and tucked it in neatly, then stooped to grab his clothes in a bundle under one arm. He caught Tristan by the hand again.

Tristan laced their fingers together and pulled Jake toward the bedroom, shivering as damp skin met the cool air. It was pleasant, after sweating it out during the workout. "This way."

"Classy," Jake approved of the sliding bedroom doors. "You can leave the doors open and have a viewing party."

Tristan burst out laughing. Jake's sense of humor was sly but dirty. "You little voyeur. Or is that exhibitionist?"

"Either/or." Jake smirked. "Can't have one without the other. Well, you can, but it's hardly ethical."

Tristan grinned. "Only ethical porn for you, huh?"

"And preferably indie studios who haven't had major scandals." Jake winked. "My collection is carefully curated."

Tristan respected that. Porn actors were already under-paid these days. Indie studios were half-run on passion instead of money now. Given his own career, the last thing Tristan wanted to do was support anyone treating their actors like shit. No doubt Jake had similar feelings about their industry.

"Neat," was all Tristan said, but he smiled broadly.

"So," Jake said, rolling his shoulders and dropping his clothes to the floor again. The thump reminded Tristan that clothes weren't the only thing in that bundle. Was Jake going to put his cock on again? "Now I just have to decide what I'm gonna do to you."

Tristan swallowed his whimper. "Anything," he admitted.

"Honestly, you could propose any kink you wanted right now and I'd fall over myself to do it."

"I like your honesty." Jake smiled at him, then gestured toward the bed. "Sit."

Tristan obediently did so, pressing his hands to the bed on either side of himself. He had a feeling he was gonna need support in a minute.

Jake unwrapped his towel and dropped it, then straddled Tristan's lap and ran his hands from his own shoulders down across his nipples and thighs. He pinched his cock between two fingers and rolled slowly, then jerked it slowly.

From this angle, Tristan got a great view of his body: strong and hairy thighs, narrow shoulders and hips, and the flushed cock that he was pulling on in slow, sensual jerks of his hand.

Tristan squirmed where he sat. He was pretty sure he wasn't supposed to follow suit and jerk off until Jake said he could do so, but he was so hard it hurt. He wanted badly to be fucked—or to fuck—or to do something, anything. Hell, he'd grind against Jake right now if that was the going option.

"Suck me," Jake whispered as he raised one foot to brace himself on the edge of the bed.

Tristan curled his fingers into the sheets and gazed up the length of Jake's body. He slowly leaned in to close his lips around Jake's cock. It took him a few moments to get used to the velvet-soft and familiar texture, but also the wrinkle of foreskin around it and the way it split underneath into more smooth skin, all the way down to his... front hole, he'd called it.

As he explored with the tip of his tongue, Jake's breathing grew heavy. Tristan paid attention to what made him give small moans of encouragement and did more of it, sucking harder on Jake and pushing his tongue against the hole until Jake rocked his hips forward.

He resisted the urge to smile. There was something wonderfully enjoyable about seeing and feeling Jake's reactions. He'd always loved giving head, and this was no exception.

For once, though, he didn't feel like he was in charge… and that made it even better.

Jake's fingertips rubbed along Tristan's scalp, and he tangled his fingers in Tristan's hair as he lazily thrust into his mouth. Tristan kept his lips pursed tightly around the shaft, gripping and pulling it whenever Jake's hips pulled backward.

That produced the best reactions of all. Jake gasped his name, his nails digging into Tristan's shoulder. Tristan did it again, bobbing his head now as he got into the rhythm.

Jake groaned, finally pulling away. He shoved Tristan's shoulders, and Tristan gasped as he hit the bed. He scooted up, not sure what was next but excited for anything that Jake might try. Jake followed, straddling his hips again.

"You're up for anything?" Jake grinned, a wickedly tempting look in his eye.

Tristan gulped. "Anything pretty vanilla. I'm not, uh…" *Experienced* wasn't the word he wanted to use, but it was true. He was used to simple in-and-out hookups. But God knew he'd had plenty of those. "Yeah," he mumbled instead of finishing the sentence.

"I'm gonna ride you," Jake told him, closing his fingers around Tristan's rock-hard shaft and gently stroking a few times.

The explosion of energy through sensitive nerve endings

made Tristan gasp. He'd been aching for attention for long enough that it took him a few seconds to adjust.

"Yes, please," Tristan managed.

"Got condoms?"

Tristan nodded and gestured toward the bedside table. As Jake crawled over to rummage for them, Tristan got a great view of his ass. "Nice," he mumbled under his breath. It was a little different, not having balls just hanging out there, but not bad.

Jake glanced back over his shoulder and grinned, then wiggled his ass. He took the lube out, too, and ran two slick fingers between his legs, staying where he was. It gave Tristan a great view of those delicate fingers pushing into himself.

God, his cock *needed* Jake right now.

Tristan scooped up the condom and took care of that himself to shave a few seconds off the waiting time until he felt himself plunging into Jake.

Jake didn't let him shift on top. When Tristan tried, Jake grinned and shoved him back to the bed, then straddled him again. "No. I'm fucking *you*."

But he was about to ride him, wasn't he? Oh, well. Higher brain function was firmly off now. Tristan gave him a loopy grin and nodded.

Whatever the hell he meant, Jake was welcome to do it. Taking him home was the best decision ever. How much hotter could he get?

CHAPTER
Five

JAKE

"I'M FUCKING *YOU*."

Tristan stared at Jake for a few moments, his brows furrowed in an adorably confused expression.

The fact that, even as an actor, he wasn't trying to disguise his confusion, made Jake smile. Tristan mirrored his grin, clearly clueless but happy to do whatever the hell Jake wanted.

It wasn't his fault, really. Jake was used to this—guys who thought that the top did the fucking and inserted their cock, and the bottom was fucked and took it.

Like the most goddamn boring under-the-covers missionary het sex.

Jake swallowed his sigh and refrained from the eye-roll. Grindr and porn instilled stupidly simplistic worldviews in guys his age. "You don't need to be on top to do the fucking," Jake added, shifting until he straddled that hard cock.

God, Tristan's dick felt good rubbing against his own. It was occasionally frustrating that his own was smaller, and it took a little effort to keep it lined up against Tristan's. Still, he found the angle quickly and thrust against Tristan, letting the lube smooth the way.

"I need you," Tristan whispered. "No matter what you wanna do to me."

God, he was adorable. He was staring at Jake like he'd never had such good sex before, and for all Jake knew, the poor guy might not have. It wasn't the first time a guy had reacted that way when Jake made them step out of the narrow little box they were used to.

Again with Grindr hookups and the skewed version of sex that the whole culture seemed to teach so many guys he'd hooked up with. They just didn't know what to do when Jake wanted to top them with his packer and harness. Or they'd insist that they were "on top" or "fucking him" when they were lying back looking clueless and Jake was in charge, just because Jake just happened to have their cock inside him.

At least Tristan was learning fast. He kept his mouth shut (except when he was sucking cock) and his mind open. Jake found that hot as hell.

Jake shifted and gripped the base of Tristan's shaft firmly as he pressed Tristan against himself.

Frontal sex wasn't always easy. After so many years on testosterone, he needed extra lube to make it work with minimal pain. But at least guys always kept that around for anal.

He was wet and ready now, and he relished the feeling of the tip pressing against his hole and slowly sliding inside. God, being filled up by a hot, hard cock never got old.

"Fuck," Tristan gasped from underneath him.

"You all right?"

Tristan's cheeks reddened and he smiled, looking shy for a moment. "Yeah."

Jake cupped Tristan's cheek with his spare hand, relying on his thigh muscles—which was always risky after a workout—to keep him steady. "Tell me if it's too tight."

Tristan shook his head, that awed expression on his face again. "It's perfect. Different, but... but good."

Jake had heard that plenty, too. He half-smiled and nodded once, then pushed himself down as far as he could handle. The initial pain was laced with pleasure, and he paused where he was for a moment before drawing himself up and pushing down again.

There it was. Within a minute, he was starting to itch for *more*, and deeper, and harder.

And as he followed his instincts, Jake enveloped Tristan's cock right to the base.

Goddamn, he was not going to last long. Having those gorgeous lips working around him, after the way they'd teased each other in the shower, had him on edge already.

It felt like he didn't have a minute to waste.

Jake set himself into a fast-paced rhythm. Their cries mingled with the slick sounds of Tristan plunging deep within Jake, and every thrust of their bodies made the tingling, aching urge to touch himself even more irresistible.

Jake gripped Tristan's shoulder with one hand and rubbed the swollen head of his cock in hard, fast circles with the other. His rhythm faltered here and there, but Tristan pushed up into him to keep them moving.

His heart pounding and body drawing tight, Jake couldn't hold back any longer. He gasped and threw his head back as he clenched around Tristan.

"Fuck," Tristan gasped from under him. Tristan gripped his hips tightly as he thrust a few more times and then shivered. His orgasm clearly hadn't been far behind.

Jake slowly slid out, giving his cock a few last tugs as he grinned at Tristan.

"That was…" Tristan trailed off and shook his head, easing the condom off himself. Jake swung his leg over Tristan to collapse next to him and give him the space to work.

"Yeah," Jake agreed. "It sure was."

"Wanna do that again sometime?" Tristan widened his eyes into a puppy-dog cute expression, and Jake laughed.

"I sense I'm being begged. I like it when you beg," Jake told him with a wink. "I'd come over again."

"Yes," Tristan hissed.

Then, he seemed to realize that he'd just propositioned Jake thirty seconds after they'd had sex. He blushed and glanced down, but that made him see Jake's hand still resting on his cock.

Tristan only blushed even harder and looked back at Jake's face again. God, for an actor, he really was showing a lot of himself.

Jake appreciated that. Unlike so many guys here, Tristan didn't have some front he was presenting—a cool guy image to maintain. He was *real* in a way Jake certainly hadn't expected.

"Hey," Jake coaxed Tristan to look at him, lifting his chin with two fingers. "It was good. Don't make a big deal of it."

"Oh, I—I wasn't." Tristan stuttered for a second, clearing his throat. "I, uh, just figured… that sounded hella uncool."

Jake laughed. "Whatever. I don't blame you for wanting another piece of this."

Plus, it was flattering. A lot of guys wanted to do him once, like a novelty. When they realized they wouldn't have a second cis-sized, flesh-and-blood penis to play with, they just assumed they were doomed to top forevermore, and they ghosted him.

Dumbasses. The sex only got better the more Jake knew someone. He and his fuck-buddies had the most fun. Not that he had any right now, but he'd had them before. People moved on too quickly from this town.

Friends with benefits suited him well, and it sounded like Tristan wanted the same thing.

"So, uh, gym again sometime?" he suggested. He could live with this if it were just sex, but he liked friendship, too. He wanted to know what to hold out hope for now, rather than waste time pining away later.

"Yeah, we could do that." Tristan's voice barely contained his excitement, and Jake smiled to himself. Then, Tristan's face fell. "So long as we… you know, in public…"

"We don't start any gay rumors about you," Jake finished.

He wasn't sure how to handle that.

On the one hand, he understood the need to be closeted. On the other… well, he'd tried to be stealth for about a year after moving to L.A. It had been nice in a way to be treated like any other guy, and to not have his identity be the first thing people thought of him, but then he'd lost an even bigger chunk of his history and himself.

Being open about it wasn't just about having other people know. It was about not having to hide part of himself, not having to think about whether something fit his "story" or not.

Jake couldn't imagine having a career that depended on his silence. He couldn't judge on an experience he'd never had.

"Is that cool with you?" Tristan asked. His expression was more guarded than it had been all afternoon.

Jake rubbed his arm gently. "Yeah. I get it. It's fine."

"Okay." Tristan's exhaled sigh was clearly relieved. "Thanks."

"Have you ever been out?" Jake didn't really know Tristan well enough to ask, and yet they'd just shared such intimacy that it didn't feel too strange.

Tristan paused and thought about it, then shook his head. "No. In high school I was pretty closeted. I've got a gay best friend—Zeph—and he knows everything. And now some of his friends know, too. Those are the guys you saw at Plus. But that's not really being out, I guess."

Jake's heart hurt for him. "You never walked down the street holding hands?"

"No." Tristan's gaze dropped again, his expression somber. "Except... with girls, on screen." His chuckle sounded distinctly bitter. "They like my leading-man looks. I'm popular with the girls. How weird is that?"

"Is it your casting agent or whatever keeping you in the closet, or a joint decision?"

"Joint," Tristan mumbled. "I don't really wanna invite trouble. It's just easier all around. He wants to make a name for me as a straight guy who's 'willing' to do gay stuff," he air-quoted.

Jake nodded. He couldn't see a future with a guy he couldn't even hold hands with in public, or kiss goodbye, or be seen with too often. That went against everything he'd built for himself in the last five years.

But Tristan was a nice guy. Genuine, kind, willing to listen and learn, and hot as sin in bed. Great sex was on the table, and maybe friendship.

Jake had learned better than to write off potential friendships in a city this big. It wasn't easy meeting people who he liked, and he wasn't throwing away the chance to get to know someone better.

Even if there was a closet door in the ceiling of their relationship, he wanted to see Tristan again, and that in itself was rare enough to explore.

"I better get going," Jake finally said, smiling to himself. "I got a shift tonight."

"Where? On a set?"

"Nah, I'm a waiter."

"Really?" Tristan blinked. "You were good at your job."

"I'm non-union. People kept telling me it would limit what jobs I could take, and I needed to be able to take anything that paid," Jake explained. "I've been doing days or weeks here and there, but not enough hours to get benefits. The day rate wasn't quite covering the bills. The bigger the production, the less they were paying me, and I wasn't union yet... and then I needed insurance for hormones and blood tests and surgery. I got a job at a restaurant. 25 hours gives me insurance benefits. Between that and short-term PA gigs now and then, it all cobbles together to make something livable."

Tristan nodded slowly. It looked like he was familiar with the story, and he probably was. Actors were often in no better a position than other film crew members when they didn't have a big name. In fact, worse in many ways... there were thousands of young kids with hopes and dreams ready to replace them at a moment's notice.

"Have you thought about going full-time as a PA?" Tristan asked.

"Maybe." Jake fidgeted with the hair on his arm, brushing his fingers one way and then the other through it. "There's a lot of work, but then I can't keep up the restaurant job. I'll have to be free at a moment's notice. So I have to make the jump fast and not look back."

Tristan nodded, his fingers tracing Jake's ribs. "That's a big decision."

"Yeah." Jake stretched and gathered his clothing. "So, off to work with me tonight."

Tristan smiled and stood up once Jake was dressed to see him to the door. "Have a good shift. Call me sometime, huh?"

"I will." Jake paused at the door as he slipped his shoes on, his gaze falling to Tristan's lips. Should he go for it?

Tristan leaned in first, and Jake met him for a quick kiss. "Bye."

"Bye," Jake managed before he headed to the elevator. He ached, but in the best possible way. Every ounce of him glowed with contentment.

His sex drive satiated, he felt much less cranky. If casual sex with Tristan helped him keep focused and energetic until he figured out this whole fertility thing, so much the better. He'd just have to make sure to use condoms, and he tended to do so anyway, so it wasn't a big change.

He was more concerned with getting his work life sorted out, savings in the bank, and a place with a second bedroom. And maybe reading some parenting manuals, and finding a support group…

Yeah, he had a long way to go before he was ready, but he felt optimistic about it.

Dr. Lume was right. It's time to go for what I want.

CHAPTER

Six

TRISTAN

"Tris! I got news for you."

A call from his agent always made it a good day. Tristan perked up as he heard Bobby's voice. "Whatcha got for me?"

"Commercial work. I know you wanted more feature films, but this will help fill the gaps."

It sure would. Tristan didn't want a reputation as a commercial actor, so it was always a risky line to walk taking too many of those jobs, but he trusted Bobby's judgment in steering his career the right direction, ultimately. "Big name?"

"Oh, yeah. A great brand. It'll look more like endorsement than desperation."

Tristan grinned. "You read my mind."

"You're doing fine," Bobby told him, but he wasn't unsympathetic. "I know this kind of work isn't the most fun, but it's better than taking a shitty movie role just to keep working. If you get known as the guy who does straight-to-DVD movies, that's not a good thing. Unless you take my audition suggestions…"

That was true, too. The last thing he needed was to be known as the guy who took ridiculous roles for movies that got panned by critics. That was a different kind of desperation altogether.

Ah, Hollywood. It could break a man's dreams if he thought he could aspire to create great artistic works, work full-time, *and* make a decent living. Luckily, Tristan had no such illusions.

"That's a yes to the commercial, then."

"Good. I'll email the details in a few minutes," Bobby told him. "In the meantime, there's a movie starting production next month, and I think you're gonna get an audition with them. I'll chase that up for you this week, too. Keep your schedule clear. The casting director liked what you did in *Summer* and wants more of that."

Tristan stifled the urge to groan. It was easily the biggest-budget movie he'd done, but one of the worst-reviewed. Cheesy and camp, the critics had said. A far cry from his leading-man image.

Especially for a straight guy, and Bobby knew damn well that he didn't want his sexuality becoming his image.

"Are you sure about that?" Tristan asked, his steps slowing.

He was out for his morning walk—the way he cooled down from his morning workout, before his morning green smoothie. There were never public places completely out of earshot of anyone who might have a scoop.

Tristan's fears had faded over the last few months of hanging out with Zeph and his friends, going out to Woody's with them, and even visiting Plus every now and then.

He wasn't a big enough name to be followed 24/7 or attract attention when he was driving around the city. But he did avoid unnecessary risks, like talking loudly about how gay he was while walking through a public park.

On the other hand, Bobby would be glad to shove him into a niche if he could. And Tristan was starting to feel worn down enough to accept it.

"Yeah. It'll get you a lot more exposure, and the director's great. If he likes you, he'll cast you in other projects in the future. And directors talk—you know how it is. The only thing is..." Bobby trailed off.

Tristan tensed up. "Yeah?"

"You might have to play gay. It's a good opportunity..."

"No." Tristan's heart jumped into his throat. "You know how I feel about that."

"A lot of guys do it these days. You'll show that you're open-minded," Bobby wheedled. "I promise you're not coming out by doing it. In fact, it's best that you don't. Looks better."

Tristan's resolve wavered. He'd trusted Bobby up until now, and there was no reason *not* to trust him now. Still, he'd spent so long carefully avoiding any hint of indiscretion that this seemed... well, batshit crazy. "Are you sure it's gonna lead to other opportunities? Or am I just gonna get typecast forever?"

"Look," Bobby told him, his voice firm. "You can't afford a drought. If you don't work for a month or two, that's not unusual at your level. Six months? A year? Your career trajectory ends there."

He was so painfully right that Tristan couldn't argue. He let out his breath and sighed, then nodded to himself. "All right. I'll audition, or whatever."

"Yes," Bobby cheered. "Good man. Okay, check your

email regularly. I'll let you know when the meeting's set up. They're delighted to have you audition."

That, at least, made Tristan smile. "Hope that holds true if I get the part."

"Come on," Bobby scoffed. "It looks good to be diverse these days."

"What do you mean?"

Bobby hesitated. "If you… well, if anything ever comes out… I wanna make sure you don't get stuck in a corner."

Tristan knew what he meant. If he got outed much later in his career—or at least, the career he hoped he was going to have—Bobby wanted him to already have good contacts who wouldn't blacklist him.

God, he hated the politics of it all. Why couldn't he just work hard, make good movies, fuck whoever he wanted, and call it a day?

"Thanks, Bobby. I'll get my schedule lined up now."

"Yep. Talk to you soon."

Tristan hung up and checked his email, wandering over to a park bench and taking a seat to block out days on his calendar.

He was lucky to be able to cobble enough work together to live in L.A., in a nice place, on his own, with healthcare… and still save up a little. That put him head-and-shoulders above a lot of actors.

Then again, he wasn't allergic to hard work, and he never brought a diva attitude to a set. Only a few people could get away with being dicks and still get work because of their name, the quality of their work, or both.

Tristan wanted to make it an easy choice to hire him, so he didn't pull that crap.

Also, Zeph would probably punch him in the nose if he

thought Tristan was being a dick or getting an ego. *Nothing like a best friend to keep you honest*, he thought, cracking a grin.

He sent Zeph a text to tell him the good news, and sure enough, his best friend suggested drinks that night to celebrate. They hadn't seen each other in a week—since he'd met Zeph at Plus, and met Jake, in fact.

He'd made time to see Jake twice more in that week, but not Zeph again. Oops. His guilt kicked in, and he couldn't say no, even if he'd wanted to.

As if reading his mind, Zeph added, *And I think you have news for me...*

About what?

The cute thing whose number you got??? You've been very quiet this week.

Tristan cracked a grin.

Drinks it is. 8? The usual place?

Fuck yeah. River's on tonight.

River was Zeph's boyfriend, and they were a drag artist who worked shows at Tristan's usual gay bar.

It was weird for Tristan to think of himself having a "usual" gay bar, given the precautions he'd taken, but he'd also made sure to specify that he had a gay best friend in interviews. Just in case he needed an excuse.

God, what he wouldn't give not to rationalize having drinks with a friend, though. Jake had been onto something when he'd asked how Tristan's life in the closet was. Pretty damn unsatisfactory, now that he'd gotten Tristan thinking about it.

But, like Jake was stuck between a rock and a hard place career-wise, so was Tristan in his own way. Risk losing his career and find another job he could somehow do? It was a huge leap to make.

Great. See you then.

He pocketed his phone again and stood up to get back to his brisk walk.

Why did the thought of telling Zeph about Jake give him butterflies? They'd always talked about their hookups—not Zeph since he'd fallen head over heels for River, but they'd shared plenty of gossip before then.

Just because they'd met up for sex three times in a week didn't mean anything.

Jake wasn't the first friends with benefits Tristan had had, despite his secrecy and attempts to keep his sex life to a minimum. And he wouldn't be the last.

No way could he be what Tristan needed, or vice versa. Tristan felt like he was lucky that Jake's orbit had intersected with his own for this long.

Wanting more was asking too much, and Tristan had learned to keep low expectations in this city.

CHAPTER
Seven

JAKE

Hey! It's Kyle. How'd you get on finding resources? Want to come out for drinks with me and the guys?

Jake hadn't been expecting another text from the friendly, energetic person he'd met at Plus. He was used to being shown pamphlets and shown the door.

A smile tugged at his lips. That was one thing he'd been missing from his life for a while: a support network. Maybe this was an opportunity to find one. Thankfully he wasn't working tonight, and he was between PA jobs.

Tristan hadn't booty-called or sexted him today, so he probably wasn't getting laid again. Just as well—Tristan seemed to have discovered an insatiable sex drive, but his own energy had been flagging.

Enough weeks had passed since his last T shot that it must have been almost gone from his body. He had an appointment in a couple weeks to check hormone levels and fertility.

That meant starting to find a sperm donor, and improving his diet, and… well, a million other things.

God, where did time go? He'd managed to spend a week just setting up his finances and trying to figure out the cost of having a kid. Results: astronomical. How the hell did anyone afford to raise them, anyway?

He couldn't really afford drinks, but he needed a listening ear. And if Tristan just so happened to be one of the guys going out… well, he'd get to see him in a friendship context, which would make a good change after a week of nonstop sex.

Not that he was complaining about nonstop sex.

I'd love that, thanks. When and where?

8, I'll text you the address.

Jake smiled when he got the message. He recognized the bar for its drag shows, though he'd only been in there a few times.

OK, see you then.

He resisted the urge to ask if Tristan was there. As far as he was concerned, if Tristan was closeted, any mention of a relationship of any kind between them was off the table. Even to his friends… just in case.

But if Tristan *did* show up at a gay bar, he wasn't the worst closet case. Jake could deal with that.

God. Why was he thinking so much about Tristan? They'd had great sex a few times. As far as Jake was concerned, that didn't mean anything.

He'd keep having sex with Tristan as long as the sex stayed good, and as long as he felt up to it. His sex drive was doing pretty damn well considering the hormonal changes that were hitting him.

It didn't mean Tristan wanted anything more. Tristan had been pretty clear that he *didn't* want more, in fact. And hiding a love interest just didn't come naturally to Jake, so it would be a pretty terrible idea to pursue more even if Tristan wanted to.

When Jake started trying to get pregnant, he was going to have to focus on himself. Then he'd have a kid to worry about, and raising them by himself. No way was he seriously dating anyone until he felt more stable in his life.

Oops. Jake was still thinking about Tristan while he figured this out, even though they were just friends with benefits. Goddamn, the man was under his skin.

Jake smiled as he shook his head ruefully. He was gonna have to distract himself by choosing an outfit, and he was going to choose something that made him look hot. If Tristan was there to admire him, that would just be a happy coincidence.

"Jake! Over here!" A group of guys waved Jake over to the booth. The first one he spotted was Tristan, even though it was Kyle calling him.

Tristan's surprise was unmistakable. He looked quickly at Kyle, and then back to Jake. He leaned in to murmur something.

Kyle wore a broad grin as he answered him, still waving Jake over.

Jake approached cautiously, offering them all a smile when he reached the booth. "Hey. Thanks for inviting me out."

"No problem." Kyle looked innocent now as he glanced between Tristan and Jake. "You two have already met, I'm sure."

Tristan's blush was obvious, and the guys around the

table laughed. Jake tried not to follow suit, but it was impossible. At least they weren't being mean about it. Just friendly teasing.

"Ah, what can I say? Hard to resist those baby blues," Jake shrugged and slid into the booth.

"I'm Zeph." That was the guy who they'd originally planned to work out with, before he'd mysteriously been absent. With Tristan looking surprised at Jake's presence, Jake was starting to suspect that everyone here was trying to set them up. "River's gonna be on stage."

"You know me, Kyle. And this is my boyfriend."

"Nic." The scruffy, dark-haired guy opposite leaned in and shook hands. Jake noticed bronze nail polish, which made him smile.

"Denver." He looked to be mid-thirties, and probably the oldest guy at the table.

He was clearly boyfriends with the youngest guy, baby-faced and beaming, who was sitting next to him and introduced himself without shaking hands, just waving. "Sam."

"I'll… try to remember all that," Jake laughed. In reality, he was pretty good at remembering people's names, even when meeting them for the first time. Being in short-term work did that. Often, most members of a film crew met for the first time when filming began, and they still had to work seamlessly together. Learning people's names helped a lot. "I'm Jake."

"You made it just in time," Sam told him.

Zeph snorted. "And then some. The show won't start until nine, at best. You should know drag shows are never, *ever* on time."

Sam laughed. "I don't get out much. You can probably tell."

"We're working on that," Denver said with a smile, squeezing Sam around the shoulders.

Despite his initial anxiety, Jake was already relaxing. Everyone here was warm and friendly in the way they interacted—none of the cattiness he feared.

From the outside, looking in, Jake had once thought gay culture was full of that kind of stuff. He got enough of it in his professional life—actors sniping at each other between takes, or producers talking about them behind their backs, and levels on levels of intricate management to make everyone work together smoothly.

Once he'd started spending time around friends and getting to know the scene, his perception had shifted totally. He wasn't afraid of it anymore.

What about Tristan? Had he even had the chance to be surrounded by like-minded people before? People who wouldn't judge him or hold his secrets over his head like threats?

It made Jake frown to think about it, but he tried not to linger on the thought. It was Tristan's choice, after all. That was what everything boiled down to—his choice to keep secrets and reap the advantages, but also accept the downsides.

"I'm gonna get a drink. Anyone else need something?"

Tristan stood up. "I'll come with."

Jake spotted a few of the other guys hiding their smiles and rolled his eyes as he headed for the bar, but he smiled, too. "Your friends are throwing you at me."

"I know," Tristan groaned. "Sorry. I didn't know they were… um, inviting you. Not that I have a problem with it," he added hastily.

"Phew." Jake grinned, letting his arm brush Tristan's as they squeezed around a table to get to the bar.

Tristan didn't jerk away like he'd expected. Instead, he touched Jake's lower back for a moment, steering him past another table.

"That would be awkward," Jake added, forcing a quick smile. "Things aren't awkward, right?" He wanted to check in, just to make sure.

Tristan shook his head. "Weirdly, it's not. You?"

"No. I like hanging out. Like I said, friends with benefits," Jake added as he leaned on the bar.

Tristan cast him a rueful smile. "Yeah. I guess I gotta work on the friendship part, then."

"This is a good start." Jake didn't want to make him feel like he wasn't doing enough.

"Yeah, it is."

They were quiet as they waited to place their drink order. Jake asked for a Coke, since he'd sworn off alcohol until after the pregnancy—however long that took.

Once they'd ordered, Jake turned to look at Tristan again. He offered a smile when Tristan caught him looking. "I like the sex, though."

Tristan blushed, which was an adorable creep of pink from his neck all the way to his ears. "Um, yeah. It's good."

Jake smirked. He'd particularly liked that they'd taken turns initiating their hookups that week. The attraction was definitely mutual. Which left them in an awkward place of trying to be friends while wanting to do so many dirty things to each other.

"Here you are." The bartender slid drinks across the bar, and Jake paid for them both before Tristan could go for his wallet.

Tristan smiled at him. "Thanks. What do I owe you?"

"A kiss later." Jake winked and looped his arm through Tristan's to lead him back to the booth. "Don't think your friends aren't watching. We can show off for them."

"I know they are," Tristan laughed. "Maybe they'll shut up about finding me a boyfriend if they think we're... you know."

Jake grinned. "A worthy cause. Always happy to help with that."

I think I'm into him, though. Sure, he'd felt fond of his fuck-buddies before, and he'd been friends with some of them. But there was an intoxicating need under his skin to get to know Tristan better, too. To hang out here and watch how he acted around friends, and see him laughing and relaxed. To talk with him about everything and see how he worked.

There was something to the whole love at first sight theory. It was a delicate silken thread between them, liable to be ruptured by the slightest disruption. Jake wanted to spin that thread and strengthen their connection before anything happened.

One thread could be snapped in the blink of an eye. The deeper the connection, and the more threads ran between them, the harder it was to pull away.

But also, the harder it was to lose Tristan when his heart and future was on the line.

He didn't know Tristan very well yet, but in intimate moments, people showed far more of themselves than they realized. Tristan was thoughtful, kind, curious, easygoing, clever, and polite. That combination was fucking rare. No wonder he wanted to know more about Tristan.

"So, how was your week?" Jake asked everyone as a way

of breaking the ice and avoiding any teasing comments when they got back to the table.

He quickly figured out what everyone did: Zeph talked about membership and class organization woes, and it turned out he ran a gym. When he asked where, he quickly found out that it was the very gym he and Tristan had gone to.

Denver ran Plus, and despite his youthful looks, Sam owned a restaurant nearby, which made him do a double-take.

Kyle worked at Plus in education, and as Denver's right-hand man. Jake had already guessed that from meeting him at the charity. His boyfriend, Nic, was a programmer, judging by his rant about debugging code.

"What about you? What do you do?"

Jake shifted as all eyes turned to him and offered an awkward smile. "Um, I work at a restaurant. Waiting tables. Not much, but it pays the bills."

"Don't put that down," Sam told him, smiling. "Good servers make the world go around!"

Jake laughed. "Yeah, well. Thanks." He did feel a little better now that he didn't have a fancy job like owning a business or working for charity. Nobody here was looking down on him for it. "And on the side, I work as a PA on film sets. Mostly movies, some commercial work. That pays better."

"Ohhh." Denver glanced between Tristan and Jake, but he didn't ask.

"Yeah, that's how we met," Tristan jumped in to explain. "A couple years back, a little indie movie."

"And then you reconnected through Plus." Denver beamed. "That's great."

Jake laughed. "Last thing I expected was to see anyone I

knew there." Then, he flushed with embarrassment as he realized how that sounded. Like he was saying he didn't think anyone he knew was HIV-positive. God, why couldn't he think before he talked? "I mean—not that I'm saying—"

"No, it's cool," Kyle chuckled. "L.A.'s a big city. I get what you mean."

Jake cast him a smile. The last thing he wanted was to make a bad impression on these guys, and by extension, Tristan. "Yeah. And I only went because my doctor referred me. Like, out of the blue. How weird is that?"

"I know how weird it is to reconnect with someone out of the blue in a city this size." Zeph cast a smug smile toward the stage, which was still empty. "That happened to River and me. And look at us now."

Nic shook his head. "They're real lovebugs."

Zeph snorted. "Really? Speaking of lovebugs? River just needed something to do after you ditched them for Nic," he told Kyle.

Kyle rolled his eyes but put his arms around Nic. "Yeah. The honeymoon phase."

Oh, God. They're all couples except Tristan and me, Jake suddenly realized. If he didn't feel awkward before, he did now. He wanted to help Tristan escape the pressure of being told he should have a boyfriend, but a little ill-timed teasing now could be disastrous.

Luckily, distraction struck a moment later.

"Oh! Show's starting!" Zeph turned eagerly to the stage, folding his hands in his lap as he waited to see his boyfriend.

Jake slowly relaxed as the lights went down. He'd survived the first conversation, at least. All he had to do was blend in and not lead Tristan on.

In the darkness, a hand touched his knee, and then ran

slowly up to take his hand. Tristan looked sideways at him and smiled tentatively as if asking permission.

Jake laced their fingers, squeezed, and smiled back. There was nothing wrong with a little affection, even if it wasn't gonna lead anywhere. Friends could hold hands, too.

It made him sad that Tristan had never held hands in public. If he wanted to try it with Jake… well, Jake was proud and happy to help him experience it for the first time.

Hell, yeah, Jake could—and would—justify this all night long.

CHAPTER

Eight

TRISTAN

IT WAS ANOTHER LONG GODDAMN DAY IN THIS LONG goddamn week.

Tristan was used to waking up early for call times and staying on set late—and his work schedule was automatically the lightest of anyone else on set.

The rest of the crew all had to set up before his first take, and break down the set or gear afterward. He tried to treat everyone with kindness and respect accordingly. But even his patience was tested when the director told them they had to reshoot the last scene one more time.

This wasn't light and easy commercial work of walking onto a screen and saying something funny. This was full-on green-screen simulated adventure sports. Which were fun at first, but when he was pretending to be thrown around in a kayak for a full minute, for the fourth time in a row and it must have been past nine at night… well, he was tired.

He was gonna throttle Bobby later.

This commercial—with the obviously-fake sports—was also unmistakably camp. Which made him worry that whatever Bobby said, he was being typecast, and that would be a trap he could never escape.

Worst of all, when he'd checked his phone on the last break, there had been a text from Jake inviting him over tonight.

If he wasn't done filming until eleven or later and had to be up early tomorrow, too… well, his booty call options this week were going to be limited. He was grumpy as hell inside, however much he hid it and kept up his goofy persona.

"Okay," Fitzgerald finally told him as he strode over.

Tristan tensed up. Either he was about to be sent home or they had another few hours ahead of them. At this point, he expected either to be possible. "What's up?"

"That's a wrap for tonight. We'll shoot the last scene tomorrow. I wanted to ask…" Fitzgerald drew him aside and lowered his voice. "Can you be a little more… well…" He meaningfully raised an eyebrow.

"More what?"

"You know. Flamboyant."

"Like… college kid in a barrel over a waterfall excitement?" Goddamn outdoor sports commercials.

"That kind of energy, yeah, yeah," Fitzgerald approved. "But more, you know. Playful. Like you don't really know what you're doing out here."

"Like I'm a dumb twink." Tristan caught himself a moment too late, his heart pounding, but Fitzgerald didn't even seem to notice the word. Was that a word everyone knew these days?

"Oh, not *that* extreme. But yeah, we want to make this seem approachable."

"Like, telling the viewer, if I can do it, so can you?" Tristan was a little less impressed with everything Fitzgerald told him. At least it was paying him well. He could do this job and then be a little choosier about his next gig.

Maybe.

"Exactly!"

"Okay." Tristan shrugged it off and put it firmly in the *think about this when I've had more wine* category in his head. For now, he was free to go.

He thanked everyone in sight, wished them a good night, tried to think less murderous thoughts, and fled for his car at the earliest opportunity.

Before he hit the road, Tristan dug his silenced phone out of his pocket.

It stayed on silent any day that he was working, from the minute he left the house for work to the minute he was back in his car. A phone ringing during a take could cost the production team hundreds or thousands of dollars. Even on vibrate, it could be audible.

He found a string of texts from Jake, and he scrolled up to read them in the right order.

Wanna come over tonight?

That was the one he'd seen earlier.

If not it's cool.

Just don't ghost me, LOL.

Fuck, I'm needy tonight. Sorry. I'm trying to shut up now! :)

...But let me know when you're free LOL.

The last one was sent just twenty minutes ago.

He quickly typed out a message in reply.

Everything OK? Just got off work.

The response was almost instant, as typing dots appeared in the little bubble on Jake's side of the screen, followed by another message.

Oh! Congrats on the booking! I didn't know you were working. Sorry. I'm OK.

Tristan's heart raced. *Still want me to come over?*

If you wanted to?

Are you asking me or agreeing?

Fine, Jake texted back with a winking face. *I'm ordering you to come over if that's what it takes. :P Here's my address.*

Tristan laughed under his breath. He could picture that bossy tone, and it did all kinds of things to him. No matter what they did together, he hadn't had bad sex with Jake yet. Jake's name gave him an subconscious thrill of pleasure now, like a Pavlovian response.

On my way... ;) Tristan answered and plugged the address into his GPS, then snapped the phone into the holder and pulled out of the parking lot.

At least ten PM had one advantage: way better traffic. In L.A., rush hour became rush morning and evening. Only late at night or very early in the morning did he have a chance of avoiding it.

Usually he went over his lines for the next day, but firstly, fuck that noise, and secondly, at least this commercial was mostly physical with little actual spoken dialog.

"Fuck that guy," he muttered under his breath as he drove on autopilot. "He just wants me to be... more gay, doesn't he?"

Which presented several problems: not only did Tristan not want to play gay on a commercial for laughs, and to imply that gay guys couldn't do anything outdoorsy, and not only did he want to avoid having his brand become *camp,* but...

Well... how could he play gay, anyway? That was what

was really sticking in his gullet about the role Bobby wanted him to take in the movie.

He was an actor. He picked up people's speech, mannerisms, habits, almost unconsciously. It was easy to blend into a crowd.

But if anything, he was a method actor. Without experiencing it himself, how could he convey what that kind of self-expression meant? And he couldn't act straight in real life and gay on screen, and take the praise for being *realistic*. God, he'd be the worst hypocrite ever.

But, then, what did *playing gay* really mean? Gay men acted all kinds of ways, and that was fine. Some, like River, were camper than summer camp, and some were the butchest guys you could imagine, and everything in between.

This was exactly why he didn't like opening that box in his head. It made him think too much, and then he started thinking about himself, and he'd done enough of that since starting to see Jake.

Yet here he was, on his way to Jake's again.

It's playing with fire, but I can't keep away. Even if I'm gonna get my fingers burned, it'll be fun for now.

He pulled up outside the apartment building and squinted to double-check the address, then found a parking spot. Everyone was home, so it took him one circle around the block before he did.

By the time he approached the front door, Jake was already waiting there for him. "Hey."

The smile on Jake's lips made Tristan smile. Even if it was late on a weeknight, and Jake was already in sweatpants and a t-shirt, he looked gorgeous—and happy to see Tristan.

"Hi," Tristan answered with a smile. Unlike those he'd

been giving people on set, this wasn't forced. He *liked* seeing Jake, and for more than sexual reasons.

So far, every time, they'd cuddled afterward for a few minutes. Talked, for at least a bit.

He knew that Jake was from somewhere further east, and that he'd left his family when they were dicks. Tristan had shared that he was in a similar boat. He had some supportive family members, at least, but not his parents.

Weirdly, they'd been more okay with him being gay than him being an actor. In any case, as far as he was concerned, his life was his own to ruin however he chose.

"How was your day? God, you look beat. I'm sorry for making you come all this way," Jake frowned.

"Nah," Tristan told him with a smile. "My place isn't even twenty minutes away."

"Still." Jake put his hand on Tristan's back and then pulled away slightly, casting him an uncertain look.

Tristan leaned into his shoulder to show him that it was okay. God, more than privacy right now, he just needed someone there to distract him from his thoughts. "I just wanted to make sure you were okay."

"I will be," Jake promised. "Just moody. Long story. Are *you* okay?"

"What? Of course. Yeah, yeah. I'm fine." Tristan couldn't stop himself before confirming at least three times that he was fine, and the more he talked, the more he blushed. "Just fine."

"Uh huh." Jake cast him an amused glance but took his hand as he led him to the staircase, and up the concrete steps two at a time. "Hot chocolate *with* Baileys it is."

"God, yes, please." Tristan's heart skipped a beat when his

hand touched Jake's. He'd wondered if he was overstepping his bounds at the club last weekend, but apparently not.

He followed Jake upstairs to the third floor, and into the little apartment. It was modest and small, but not shabby. They passed by a few doors close to the front door, and into a living room area. A kitchen was tucked into a niche in the wall.

"Not a bad place. On your own?"

"Yep." Jake smiled at him. "I'm tired of roommates. If it's a little crappy, I don't care."

Tristan completely understood. The tradeoff between a nice place and privacy was a classic choice. Frankly, if he didn't get his ass into gear, he wasn't going to be able to afford his current place anyway without dipping into savings… but that was a problem for Future Tristan.

Tonight Tristan was more concerned with crashing on the couch, watching Jake flit around the kitchen making them mugs of hot chocolate. He smiled as he glanced around the living room. He didn't want to feel like he was spying on Jake, but he was curious.

Hints of Jake's personality shone through even at a quick glance: a world map on the wall, a small army of cushions lined up along the back of the couch, and coffee table books about forests and tiny homes.

Tristan smiled as Jake crashed next to him, carefully balancing a cup in each hand. He handed a mug to Tristan and held his own out to clink. "Cheers."

"To the healing power of chocolate." Tristan grinned and sipped, then moaned his appreciation for the hot mug of liquid heaven in his hands. "God. Thanks. This was just what I needed."

"I could tell." Jake beamed. "Serious chocolate deficiency

shouldn't go untreated. And I can't drink right now anyway. Someone should use up the sad, neglected bottle of Bailey's."

Tristan was already unwinding and laughing as Jake teased him. "Yeah, I'll follow your prescription."

Jake turned sideways and pulled his legs up under himself, then balanced a cushion on his knees and propped his mug on it. "So, what's up?"

"Oh, I've been filming a commercial for the last few days. We wrap it up tomorrow."

"Commercials," Jake echoed approvingly. "Those are good work. At least on our side of the industry, they pay better than most jobs."

"Yeah…" Tristan trailed off. He shouldn't let it bother him, he knew. There was no point in getting angry at some heavyhanded and slightly homophobic creative direction. He'd endured worse.

"But?" Jake's gaze was perceptive.

"But…" Tristan trailed off, and then shook his head. "He wants me to be more flamboyant and less competent at the outdoors."

Jake snorted. "Classy."

"Yeah. I could have seen that coming, in retrospect."

"How are you gonna handle it?"

Another good question. Jake was full of them. "I don't know," Tristan admitted. "I think I'll suck it up and get the job done. But, you know, it's this kind of crap that burns me out."

Jake's gaze sharpened again. "Are you happy with your career?"

"Yeah." Tristan had said so for so long that he wasn't really sure anymore. He paused and frowned. "Maybe."

Jake nodded. "Love to hate it, or hate that you love it?"

"Ouch." Tristan chuckled, cradling his mug by his chest and sipping a few times as he thought about it. "I hate that I love it. It feels like it's got me by the balls." It was the first time he'd really thought about that, let alone said it out loud, and he reeled as he did so.

"Hmm." Jake didn't seem in a rush to diagnose or fix his problem. He let it stay hanging in the air between them as he leaned back and sipped from his mug. "You look... surprised."

"I am." Tristan laughed abruptly and touched Jake's knee —the sliver of it he could see under the pillow. "Sorry. I don't wanna make you play psychotherapist."

Jake shook his head. "It's fine," he said with a gentle smile.

There was something in the air between them, or perhaps around them. A cocoon of sorts, keeping the rest of the world and all their goddamn problems out. It was that late-night spell between lovers, or friends, or just two souls that needed to meet at that moment in time and share something special.

Something that they'd never forget.

The two of them, all alone save for their own thoughts and fears, memories and dreams.

Jake's hand slid into Tristan's, and they held eye contact for a few moments. Somehow, though, Tristan didn't feel the need to kiss him to prove anything. It felt like they were beyond that stage of intimacy, without even needing words to confirm it.

"Are you—"

"What—"

They started speaking at the same time, then tripped over their own tongues to gesture the other one to go ahead instead. They shared a laugh, and finally, Tristan felt compelled to speak.

"Are you happy working in the industry? I mean, I know it's only part-time, but... is that what you want to do more of?"

Jake blew out a little sigh and laughed. "I don't know. It's not stable work, and it's physically demanding. I have some things I want to do and it wouldn't be... the best idea." He frowned. "I enjoy it, but it's not my life's work."

"What is?"

"Now you're getting into real talk," Jake said. He grinned as he sipped his hot chocolate, then set the mug aside and kicked the pillow away to scoot closer to Tristan. "I want a family, someday. Maybe a boyfriend. I don't know. But a kid. I've always wanted that. I thought for a long time I couldn't have one, but... one way or another, that's what I want."

Tristan blinked a few times. "Wow. Okay. You know what you want. I was expecting a little more *I don't know, I need to go practice yoga in India and find myself.*"

Jake snorted with laughter. "Most people don't need that. They just need to learn to find the small good things right here."

"You're gonna be good at that whole parenting thing," Tristan told him with a chuckle. "You have the wisdom down pat. What about the wisecracks?"

"Don't get me started," Jake warned. "Not unless you're really willing to open that Pandora's box."

Tristan winked. "Is that a challenge?"

Jake elbowed him but settled against his side. "What about you? Besides acting, what's your ideal life like?"

"I always thought it was out here being a big-name star, but the more I think about it, the less I like that idea. I'm already afraid of the spotlight, of being outed." Tristan wasn't afraid to speak so frankly—not to Jake. "It would make all of that worse. Unless I came out. But I'd have to be a big enough name for that, and even then... everyone's told me not to. Except my agent, who wants me to be more gay. I don't know who to listen to."

"Does what you're doing now feel right?"

"For now, yeah. Forever? I don't think so." Tristan frowned. "I've always listened a little too much to authority."

Jake squeezed his fingers, lacing them tightly. "A lot of people do. Most of us, really. I think it's the default, unless you had really rebellious parents, or... I don't know, you're pushed into it. Or you've had to fight for your right to exist."

Tristan quietly nodded. Maybe that was part of his attraction to Jake: how fiercely unapologetic he was for *who* he was. Tristan drew a breath and let it out, then rested his head on Jake's shoulder. He felt safe talking to him in a way he hadn't experienced before, outside of Zeph.

But Zeph was a friend. This? This was more than that.

He couldn't put words to the attraction without stopping to think about it, and if he did that, he might just lose his grip and fall towards Jake.

"I guess if I did something else, I'd have to get trained in it." Tristan smiled ruefully. "I've had so much acting training that it feels like a waste."

"Sunk cost fallacy," Jake said succinctly. When Tristan just blinked at him, Jake explained. "When you've already spent time or energy or money on something, you'll keep spending because you feel like it's a waste of what you've already spent. That's how companies get away, with like..." He looked around, and then his eyes lit up. "Laptops!"

Watching him get passionate about explaining this was so

adorable that it took Tristan some effort to listen to what he was saying. "Laptops?"

"You know how, like, the screen will break? And then the power adapter? And then the keyboard? And you'll pay a couple hundred bucks and get it fixed over and over? And if you do the math, you've spent more on parts than you did on the damn thing in the first place. But you feel like you've wasted both the original investment *and* money on all the parts you've fixed if you don't stick with it."

Tristan nodded. "But it *would* be a waste, wouldn't it?"

"No. That money's already gone. They call that throwing good money after bad. Same with your time or energy," Jake said.

Tristan rubbed his thumb along the side of Jake's hand as he turned the ideas over in his head.

"Plus," Jake added, squeezing his hand until he looked, "nothing you do is a waste. You had a great time. You did good work. If you move on, or if you switch to the stage, or only commercials, or whatever the hell you do… that doesn't mean the other stuff you did wasn't worth it."

Tristan grinned. "Yes, Yoda."

"Shut up." Jake looked embarrassed now.

Tristan didn't want him feeling bad, so he hurried to add, "You're right, though. I'm compelled to accept the words of wisdom. Should I wax on and off?"

Jake's embarrassment gave way to laughter again. "I'm just saying."

"You're smart and put-together. It's kind of intimidating," Tristan admitted.

"You've got a better house, though. And career. I'm nowhere near ready for anything I want in life," Jake told him.

Tristan snorted. "It's not about that."

"Oh, but it is." Jake was playing with Tristan's fingers now, running his fingers along each one and touching the back of his hand. Perhaps as an excuse for looking down at his hand, rather than meeting his gaze.

Tristan nearly held his breath as he waited for Jake to say more. He sensed he was at the edge of something delicate here—though they'd been treading carefully all evening.

"It's like… I'm twenty-seven. My mom was four years younger when she had me. I've barely got my feet under me." Jake frowned at Tristan's hand, and he slowly looked up at him. "Sorry. I'm just hormonal."

"Hey, it's okay." Tristan shook his head. "Wanting a family, feeling worried about the future… all that stuff is universal."

"Is it?"

"Yeah. I've often wondered when the hell I'll grow up and stop chasing this fairytale."

Jake's brows climbed. "Really? But you're… successful."

"From a certain vantage point, yeah. You know when you're climbing a mountain?"

Jake snorted. "Like you'd catch me on a mountain. But yeah?"

"You feel like you're gonna get to the top, and then you get over the hill and you realize there's another *real* mountain top, you're not there yet. And sometimes you get there and that's fake, too."

"I see where you're going with that." Jake laughed quietly.

Tristan sighed and shrugged. "I don't know. I love what I do, when I get to do it. I work my ass off, and I love that."

"I remember that," Jake told him with a smile. "Not all the actors I've worked with do."

"Yeah. That's why I've managed to do what I have done, at

least," Tristan told him. "Directors who want someone who's easy to work with. And then I can learn to be good at it as I go."

"Now who's wise?"

"Ah, it gets better." Tristan smirked and tapped Jake's nose, which earned him a yelp and a swat. He laughed. "See, you might be worried about starting a family and waiting around too late, but... you just need to get started. Figure it out as you go. Right?"

Hopefully that advice was right. He wasn't a parent. He knew plenty of parents, but mostly more successful actors, or those with spouses who had day jobs to cover their acting hobby.

But he was pretty sure nobody was supposed to know what they were doing at first. That was the classic refrain, anyway.

"I *am* getting started," Jake told him. He scooted closer, and Tristan wrapped an arm around his shoulders. Jake picked up Tristan's other hand and started rubbing that one now, pressing his cheek into Tristan's shoulder. "I've stopped hormones. I'm gonna see if my cycle comes back, and if I can still get pregnant, and... figure out a job, and a better place to live... and find a donor. I don't think a sperm bank would work with me. Well, I know they wouldn't."

Whoa. That was a lot to take in at once. Tristan blinked a few times at him, and his admiration only grew. "As a single dad?"

"Sure," Jake said and grinned. "No parenting disputes."

Tristan cracked a smile. "It's a lot of work to be a single parent, but I think you'll be fine."

"Thanks."

"No, really." Tristan squeezed him around the shoulders.

"I know we've only known each other for a few weeks, but… you *do* have your shit together. You make me think and teach me things. You're willing to work hard to support your family, I can tell that right away. If you don't know all the details… well, they'll get filled in later."

Jake finally leaned in to kiss him. Plain as day, it was a nonverbal *thank you*. Tristan smiled and cupped Jake's cheek as he kissed him back, letting them have this sweet, tender moment together.

"All right," Jake murmured. "You're right. I'll figure it out as I go… and so will you. But I wanted to tell you that. Even if we're using condoms, I thought you should know. It could take a while for my fertility to return, but there's that chance."

Tristan appreciated Jake even more. "That's very respectful. See? Good dad material," he teased. He squeezed Jake's shoulder and settled down again, then hummed. "And you want to be the one… carrying the baby?" He didn't really know how to talk about it, but so far, he hadn't horribly offended Jake. He was willing to give it a try.

"Yeah. I worried for a while that it was too weird, that I wasn't supposed to. But I think it's just parenting instinct. Wanting biological kids. And since I can't make sperm…"

Tristan shook his head. "No, I get it." If he were honest, he'd felt that itch, too. "I mean, I can't imagine what it's like to look at… you know, nine months of all *that*… but a lot of people want kids. I don't think that's a gender thing at all."

Jake sighed and snuggled into him. It was a distinctly comfortable movement, and it made Tristan smile that Jake felt so good with him. "Yeah," Jake murmured. "Exactly. I want all those organs out eventually, but I want kids first. And egg freezing is horrible."

"Is it?" Tristan could honestly say he knew nothing at all about it.

"Oh, yeah. And even then, there's no guarantees it would work, and I'd have to find someone else to carry the baby, and… just… no. If I can do it, it would make life a lot easier. No getting doctors involved until I have to."

There was something hiding in the undertones of his voice there. Tristan could hear it. Maybe fear? Resentment? Anxiety? All perfectly understandable emotions.

"I get that," Tristan murmured. "It's gotta be a big thing to think about."

"Understatement." Jake laughed. "Anyway, that's why I'm all hormonal, so… sorry."

Tristan shook his head. "No, don't apologize. I get emotional too. All of us are like… big meat sacks driven around by hormones and feelings and instinct. We all have our *beep beep, hormonal road rage* moments. How the hell are we all still alive?"

Jake broke out laughing and doubled over, covering his face. "It's true."

Seeing Jake lighten up made Tristan grin. "Anyway, we should probably… I mean, I should get to sleep."

"It's late. You wanna stay over?"

"Call time is early," Tristan warned, but his heart lifted with hope.

He didn't know why, but he wanted company that night. Maybe because they'd talked about so many vulnerable things, and it felt like the middle of the night, and he just wanted to curl up with Jake and sleep off this strange fog of emotional closeness.

Jake grinned. "I'm used to that. I'll set an alarm for you."

"Then yeah," Tristan told him softly, rubbing his back. "I'd love to stay."

Jake smiled and stood up, offering him a hand. "Bedroom's this way."

One thing was for sure: the more he got to know Jake, the more he *wanted* to get to know him. He was falling toward him, and he couldn't stop himself.

CHAPTER
Nine

JAKE

WAKING UP IN TRISTAN'S ARMS MADE JAKE SMILE, NO MATTER what hour the alarm was going off.

"Oh, God," Tristan mumbled behind his neck, pressing his forehead into the back of Jake's neck. "Is it morning already?"

Jake laughed quietly as he rubbed Tristan's arm, then rolled over to turn the alarm off. "Afraid so."

He had been described as an annoyingly cheerful morning person before, but he'd learned to rein it in. Too many people had threatened to punch him for being bright and chirpy before they'd had caffeine.

"Fine," Tristan grumbled. "But I won't like it."

Jake grinned to himself, then schooled his expression into sympathy as he rolled over to face Tristan. "I could improve your morning."

Ding! He practically heard the cartoon sound and saw the lightbulb over Tristan's head as interest brightened his sleepy eyes and downturned mouth. "Oh?"

Jake hummed, and then scooted his way down Tristan's body, pulling the sheet over his head when he reached his waist. A whole blanket on top would make him overheat, but there were few things sexier than the sight of a sheet bobbing over your dick.

Morning wood greeted him, and Jake grinned. Half of his work was already done. He breathed across the tip gently, until Tristan started squirming.

"Oh, man. You *can* brighten my day."

Jake chuckled, and then licked the tip slowly. He took the velvet-soft weight into his mouth, bobbing his head down at just the right angle to take it to the back of his throat.

Yeah, he was good at giving head, and he was proud of it. He liked making guys feel good, and he'd even learned to live with the fact that he rarely got as good head in return.

Tristan tried, though, bless him. He was getting better. With a little training, he was almost boyfriend material.

Jake choked. *When was the last time I thought that about anyone?*

Tristan gasped and groaned sharply at the sound. Of course it was sexy to hear. It was a compliment, after all.

Jake stifled his smile and deliberately choked a few more times, just a little, as he kept going.

"Baby, I'm nearly there," Tristan warned in a whisper. "So damn sensitive in the morning."

As far as Jake was concerned, Tristan didn't need to explain himself. He'd take it as a compliment.

He moaned his encouragement, and Tristan's hot load went straight down his throat. Maybe he shouldn't have done it, but he'd deal with it later. Oral was pretty low-risk, as far as risks went.

And he hadn't slept with anyone else in, like, a month. That was practically commitment as far as he was concerned.

"Oh, man. You're the hottest guy I've ever known." Tristan wasn't even saying it with that overly eager *see? I'm gendering you right!* tone he was used to. Which meant that Jake could just relax and enjoy the compliment.

Or squirm at it, really. He hardly knew what to do when he wasn't on-guard for backhanded compliments.

Jake knew he was blushing as he poked his head out from under the sheet for fresh, cool air. At least he could blame it on the heat under the sheets. "Yeah." He tried to play it cool.

Tristan smiled and pulled him up by the arms until he lay on Tristan's chest, their foreheads bumping. Jake squeaked with surprise.

Tristan laughed. "Sorry."

"Oh, I'll let you get away with the manhandling. Just this once," Jake teased. He rolled off and checked the clock. "What time do you have to get going?"

Tristan followed his gaze and then gasped, sitting straight upright. "Shit."

Jake rolled off him and pointed him to the shower. "That way. I think I've got something to fit you."

"I'll only be in it until I get to set anyway. I can bring your clothes back," Tristan called as he sprinted.

"No problem." Jake flopped back against the pillows and sighed to himself as he shoved his underwear down, then pinched his cock between two fingers and started jerking off as the shower ran.

An all-too-familiar scenario, and one he'd avoided with Tristan until now. Oh, well. He couldn't have it all.

By the time Tristan was out, Jake had gotten off, and he was shoving on sweatpants for the morning as he laid out clothes that were just a bit too big for him.

"You working today?" Tristan hopped from foot to foot as

he pulled on socks, and Jake reached out to steady him with a hand on his arm.

"Yeah. Later, at the restaurant."

"Until late?"

"I'm closing."

"Huh. Okay. I'll text when I'm done, then," Tristan told him. "I owe you one." Jake waved him off, but Tristan added, "Seriously," and pulled him in for a quick kiss before he sprinted for the door.

"Bye!"

"Have a good day!"

With that, the door closed, and Jake leaned against the wall of his bedroom to try to figure out how he felt.

"You look like the cat who got the cream."

Amanda always saw through him. They were just casual work friends—coworkers who swapped jokes—but Jake was glad for her company. She'd quickly spotted him and taken him under her wing when he started working there.

When they had a slow shift, they traded jokes and sometimes stories. After they closed the place, the raunchier stories came out. Or back in the kitchen—the kitchen staff loved a good gossip. He could see Milo listening in as he chopped lemon slices.

"Uh." Jake looked for an escape, but he had two tables, and neither of them needed *another* water refill. The supper rush had long since passed, leaving just the last few stragglers.

Good thing, too. His energy was pretty damn low. It felt

like dragging himself through molasses just to get dressed and get to work on time, let alone do anything *at* work.

He'd forgotten what this felt like, since teaching himself to self-inject his T. No more appointment gaps between nurse-administered injections.

Amanda knew she had him cornered. She folded her arms and grinned. "No denying it. Spill. Is it a boy?"

Jake couldn't stop his blush. Fuck. Why did he always react so easily? It was not a well-adapted trait for survival of embarrassing situations and interrogation.

"It is!" Amanda's brows shot up. "Holy crap. How long now?"

The chopping stopped, and Milo poked his head around the corner to watch them.

Jake waved at them both. "Gossips, both of you. A week or two, I dunno. Super-casual, that's all."

"But you like him. You haven't told me about a boy since… like… ages ago." Amanda twirled her hair around her pen and tucked it behind her ear again as she thought. "The one who turned out to be a dick."

"Could be any of 'em," Jake muttered, making her grin. His last boyfriend had been over a year ago. He'd had a string of three-month relationships before one thing or another got in the way. It wasn't exactly a glowing track record on his part.

"Is he cute? What's his name?"

Jake bit his lip and shook his head. "Can't say."

"You don't *know* his name?" Milo piped up, no longer bothering to pretend he wasn't listening.

Jake snorted and sank onto the stool by the POS system. None of those checks were close to ready to print. Could he escape to unload the dishwasher? "Ha ha. No. I can't say. He's… closeted."

Amanda hissed through clenched teeth, her brows knitting together. "Wow. And you're… you. You're okay with that?"

"Yeah." Jake offered a smile. "Nobody can decide that kind of stuff for anyone else. He feels safer that way."

"*Is* he?"

Jake wasn't sure, honestly. "I mean, I hated the closet myself… but it's a different kind of thing for me. And I've never had much choice but to be open gender-wise, so… sexuality was almost easy after that. It all came together, at once. I don't know what it's like to grow up gay. Who am I to argue?"

"You were still gay before, um," Amanda fumbled. "Before transition."

"Right," Jake agreed, offering a smile to reassure her that she'd used the right word. "But I didn't always know. I wasn't a little seven-year-old boy wanting to kiss other boys on the playground. Yeah, some gay trans guys do feel like they grew up gay. Not me, though. It's just a different experience."

"And I haven't been kept out of STEM programs for being a girl, but some girls are," Amanda pointed out, then jerked a thumb at Milo. "He's a gay chef. That's a hard business, too. We all have different experiences. But if you end up hiding away when you're not used to it…"

"Oh, no," Jake reassured her, even though doubt nibbled at his thoughts. "I wouldn't let that happen."

The door opened, and he hurried to the front to escape the worry that he *might* just let Tristan hide him away from the world, if just to be with him.

He couldn't process what he was seeing for a few seconds.

Tristan stood there, a red rose in his hand.

Oh, God. He's got a wife. He just came from a date. He's on his way to see someone. All of those possibilities occurred to him before the one easiest explanation that presented itself.

Or, rather, was presented when Tristan reached out to offer him the rose.

"Um." Jake's voice cracked. He felt dizzy as he took the stem of the rose, then glanced down at it and up at Tristan a few times.

Tristan cleared his throat. "That's to say sorry for running out on you this morning. And to say... um, thanks for the talk last night. And thanks for everything. Is it okay for me to come by?"

Tristan's confidence seemed to fade as he looked at Jake, replaced by a shy kind of charm he hadn't seen before.

Jake kind of hoped that meant he was feeling the same way that he felt about Tristan, but he didn't want to count on it. And he especially didn't want to ask. Not yet.

Not so soon.

"Yeah, sure," Jake said with a smile. Other waiters had their boyfriends and girlfriends and whatever come by. It wasn't a big deal. "If you don't mind. But if you've given me... and my coworkers see..."

"I remember last night's talk," Tristan said quietly. "It doesn't really matter how big a name I am. There will never be a good time to make the big reveal. I don't want to get to the top of my field and then find out who doesn't really have my back. So I'm not going to do any Pride floats, but I'm not hiding it, either. That's a miserable life. Can I just grab a table and order cheesecake and stare adoringly at you?"

"O-Of course. Yeah. Yes. Of course. Sorry." Jake snapped into hosting mode and brought him to a quiet table in the corner, well aware of the few people in the restaurant glancing at the rose in his hands, and the man who was with him. His cheeks were bright red, he knew it.

At least he didn't have to tell Tristan that he'd been gossiping about him just a minute ago. Tristan was comfortable with his coworkers guessing, or he wouldn't have come here—especially not bearing flowers.

"I can hold onto that until you're done your shift, if you want," Tristan offered with a smile. "If I can lure you back to my place tonight..."

Jake wasn't in until lunchtime tomorrow, and he suspected Amanda would fall over herself to pick up his shift if he so much as hinted that he wanted the day off, too. He fought back a smile when he glanced over his shoulder and saw her quickly walking the other way.

"Okay. But I've got a doctor's appointment in the morning."

Tristan's face fell, but he nodded. "If you need to take off early, you can. God knows I did today," he laughed.

"We'll figure it out." Jake set the rose on the table and tried desperately to remember his serving protocols. "So, um, the dessert menu..."

"Strawberry cheesecake," Tristan told him with a broad smile. "I looked up the menu online."

"O-Oh. Cool. And to drink?"

"I'll take a Diet Coke."

Jake nodded quickly. "Got it." He strode for the kitchen to enter the order, and no sooner than he'd tapped his ID into the computer than Amanda appeared at his elbow.

"Is *that* him?" she hissed. "Holy shit, he's hot!"

Jake winked. "Remember what I said. I can't confirm or deny anything."

"Oh, my God. You need to date this man," Amanda told him, and her face settled into alarming determination. "He brought you a flower. If you could see your face right now, hon. That man is your dreamboat."

"Yeah, well," Jake mumbled. He couldn't very well confess love to Tristan while they were still doing… whatever they were doing right now. "It's complicated."

"Mmm." Amanda arched an eyebrow and wordlessly disappeared to the kitchen. Milo poked his head around the corner to spy on Tristan's table a minute later.

Jake stifled his laugh and covered his face.

Oh, man. With all eyes on them, it was going to be a long damn hour before the end of his shift.

CHAPTER

Ten

TRISTAN

"I hope I didn't make things awkward tonight."

They walked hand-in-hand toward Tristan's car, and it was a strange feeling. Tristan had never held hands with someone he liked before—not off-screen, anyway.

It was warmer and sweatier than he'd imagined, but it also made his whole world somehow narrow to Jake. Like Jake was the only person who mattered to him, and in some ways, he could see that becoming true.

Despite himself, he kind of wanted people to see him on Jake's arm. Like he was showing him off.

He wanted Jake to be his.

God, they were going to have to talk out what this was between them soon—hopefully tonight.

"No, no," Jake assured him. "It was fine. As long as you're comfortable with it."

"I don't know what I'm comfortable with anymore," Tristan admitted with a small smile. "I've been thinking about everything way too much. I'm not that kind of guy."

"You're a feeler. I like that." Jake gave him a smile and

squeezed his hand, then let go when they got to Tristan's car. "So, should I follow you back, or…?"

"Fuck it. We'll take my car. I'll drop you off here to get it, or I'll drive you to your appointment tomorrow, I don't mind." Tristan shook his head, watching Jake pat down his pockets. "Unless… is this parking lot safe overnight?"

"Yeah, security knows my car. They won't tow me." Jake grinned at Tristan. "You just don't want to take your hands off me, that's the problem."

Tristan pretended to growl and pushed Jake up against the hood of the car. "You bet."

Jake giggled and shoved his chest. "Amanda will be out any minute."

"So proper," Tristan pretended to sigh and roll his eyes, keeping their bodies pressed together. "Next, you'll want to take me to dinner first. But cheesecake is close enough, right?" Jake had treated him to it, too, despite Tristan trying his hardest to pay.

"Not sure what the chivalry handbook says about that." Jake smirked up at him, his charm at full blast. "But it definitely doesn't include screwing in a restaurant parking lot."

"Fuck that manual, then."

"I was thinking of more manual fucking," Jake whispered and squeezed Tristan's ass. "Get me to your place." As always, the confidence Jake radiated made Tristan instinctively respond.

Tristan winked. "Oooh. Yes, sir. If you're in a rush, I'm sure I can oblige."

This was a whole new kind of excitement for him. He'd never let himself sleep with the same guy so often, and part of him had expected the novelty to wear off. After all, they already knew each other's bodies. They'd fooled around pretty much every way they could, with one glaring exception.

And Tristan distinctly felt it pressing into him.

"Are you wearing a... I mean, do you have..." Tristan fumbled for the right words, not wanting to kill the mood.

Jake pressed against Tristan's thigh, the bulge suddenly obvious. Feeling him there ignited sparks of expectation under Tristan's skin. "I'm packing hard, yeah. I haven't had a turn yet, and I plan to change that."

"Let's go," Tristan choked out, his voice hoarse all of a sudden. He was stirring to life in his jeans, his cock hot and his thoughts hotter.

"Now who's in a rush?" Jake was in no hurry to ease away from the car, but he finally sauntered around to the passenger side, grinning like the cat who got the cream. Or was about to, anyway.

Tristan fumbled with the door handle. Goddamn, driving with a hard-on was awkward, but he had the suspicion Jake wasn't going to give him a break.

Sure enough, once the car was started, Jake reached over the center console to put a hand on Tristan's thigh.

Just that—he didn't run his fingers up along sensitive skin, he didn't even squeeze... but that much was enough to make Tristan stop breathing for a few seconds.

How had Jake managed to squirm his adorable little way into Tristan's heart, and the center of all his fantasies, and his bed? But there he was, trying to apply logic again.

Feelings, though... feelings were leading him straight down the path to more feelings. And then the commitment kind of feelings.

Jake was changing everything in ways he didn't even

know yet. Tristan laughed under his breath as he pulled onto the road.

"Hm?" Jake questioned. His hum was soft, but it was distinct nonetheless.

Without even the radio on, there was just road noise and… something undefinable between them. Tristan could almost hear it. Like a buzz, but not in the air. It was under his skin, simultaneously calming the stress he hadn't even been aware of and waking up nerves he hadn't known existed before Jake.

It was hard to think how to explain it, so Tristan just huffed a quick chuckle. "I can't. It's just… being around you is too good."

Jake smiled softly and squeezed Tristan's knee. "Yeah. I know that feeling."

The drive seemed quicker than he'd expected as they made small talk about Tristan's latest gym foray, and Jake's coworkers. Everything Tristan said seemed to pass in one of Jake's ears and out the other, the conversation bouncing between subjects; even so, there was a certain way Jake watched him that told him Jake wasn't just hearing him… he was listening.

It seemed like he'd barely blinked before they were inside, shrugging off their shoes. Jake caught Tristan's hand before he could pull his shirt off. "I want that pleasure."

A few little words, and the fire was burning brightly again under Tristan's skin. He needed to be needed, and Jake more than rose to the occasion.

"I've been looking forward to this," Jake murmured, grinning up at him.

"Were you packing hard at work?"

"No. I leave a rod in the glovebox, in case of emergencies. I snuck out to get it."

"A rod..." Tristan trailed off, glancing down at Jake's bulge.

"You know what? You'll see in a minute," Jake said with a grin. "Spare me the sex ed role."

"You can teach me by doing, not telling."

Tristan slid the bedroom door shut, which always made the place feel cozy. Warm. Inviting. Just the two of them, and these four walls. When they couldn't even see the rest of the apartment, let alone the rest of the world, Tristan liked it.

"It's been too damn long," Tristan complained. They hadn't fucked last night, and that had felt like the right choice, but... he'd missed it.

"Days and days," Jake teased as his gaze roved up and down Tristan's body. "Like three whole days, right?"

Tristan laughed, and just then, Jake grabbed him by the shirt. His laugh faded as arousal took the place of amusement.

Jake steered him over to the bed, his fingers stretching the fabric. God, he was stronger than he looked.

Tristan obediently sat when he was pushed down, and then he gasped as he found himself stripped of his t-shirt in one fluid move. "Oh, hello."

"You've been sitting there, eyeing me up from your booth, all night." Jake clicked his tongue. "Making it hard to focus on work."

"Was I making you hard?" Tristan leaned back, pressing his palms into the bed and trying for an innocent smile. "I had no idea."

"The way you ate that cheesecake is at odds with that

expression," Jake said as he poked Tristan's chest with his finger, but he was grinning.

Tristan spread his knees so Jake could get closer, but he still stood just far enough away that their legs didn't touch. The distance between them made him ache, and he itched to close it somehow. He tried cocking his head in a come-hither expression.

Jake just grinned. "I see you've got a Bluetooth speaker over there." He swayed back and forth, tugging at his own clothes.

"Yeah. Why—ohhh." Tristan bit his tongue, not wanting to jinx himself. If he was about to get a striptease, he was going to enjoy every damn moment of it.

Within a minute, Jake had his phone connected and was playing a low, thumpy song Tristan recognized from his rare club outings. Something with a beat he could move to.

He shimmied closer and caught Tristan's eye before peeling his shirt off. One button at a time, he exposed more skin until his shirt was open, and then turned around to give Tristan a view of his ass.

He wasn't a professional dancer, but he moved with the kind of certainty of a man who knew his body inside and out, and knew what he liked, and knew what other guys liked about him.

It was utterly intoxicating. Tristan was supposed to be the one with all the sex appeal—the yearned-after movie star—and yet it was Jake who was unquestionably commanding every ounce of attention here.

"You're magnetic," Tristan whispered. "You know that aura belongs in front of a camera, not behind it?"

Jake winked and shook his head, not accepting the compliment but not exactly shooting it down, either. "You'd find me in the catering tent before you found me in front of a camera, Tris."

The nickname made Tristan beam. Only his good friends called him that, and Jake had more than earned that right. "Yeah."

He couldn't think of anything more intelligent to say, because Jake had started to slide his shirt off. When he turned around again, his chest was at eye-level, muscled and gleaming in the bedroom lamplight.

"You're gorgeous," Tristan murmured, his lips curling up into a broad smile. He couldn't stop himself—either from smiling at the way his every ounce of attention was focused on Jake, or from commenting on it.

Jake grinned. "Wait until you see my cock." He swayed his hips as he unzipped his pants.

"I already know it's gorgeous."

"Oh, this is a different cock," Jake told him with a playfulness that made Tristan burst out laughing.

"You get to just swap dicks whenever you like. Do you know how many guys would kill to be able to do that? Have a little one for skinny jeans, and a big one for those XL nights..."

"I know exactly how many guys would kill for that," Jake smirked. "Or to be on the receiving end of that. And tonight," Jake murmured, "that's you."

Fuck. Tristan kind of loved him. "It's me," he echoed dumbly. Holy crap, had Jake completely addled his brains? Apparently so, because all he could think of was that response.

Jake slid his trousers down and stepped out of them, and the outline of his cock was even more apparent as he stepped close, standing between Tristan's legs at last.

"It's going to be a little different than a flesh-and-blood penis."

"And you're a little different than most guys." Jake recoiled for a moment, his expression guarded, and Tristan realized how that sounded. Tristan hastily added, "In a good way. Jesus, I don't doubt that. I can't remember the last time I had a guy more than once."

Jake relaxed again and smiled back. "Yeah. You're different, too. And I can't figure it out. Or you out, really."

"But you want to try?"

"I want to fuck you tonight," Jake said and smirked. "We'll see about after that."

Tristan was practically vibrating from the skin contact, and Jake's thighs pressing his legs apart. He leaned in to press kisses along Jake's stomach, bending down until he was kissing fabric.

One of Jake's hands was suddenly in his hair, gripping tightly.

Tristan moaned his approval and arousal, lipping the outline of the shaft and gazing up at him. The angle was awkward, but totally worth it to see the look on his face.

Jake was hungry, and more than ever before, Tristan wanted him. If all Jake could do was chew him up and spit him out, Tristan was okay with that. It was his own damn fault for wanting to have his cake and eat it too.

Fuck. Don't think about that. Don't think at all. Just do.

Tristan followed instinct and blind desire as he pulled Jake's underwear down slowly, careful to leave the jock strap on. The hard cock inside was curved slightly, tucked against one leg.

Jake slid a hand into his field of vision and bent his shaft up. It clicked ever so faintly as he did so, holding in place when he'd bent it up. Tristan immediately understood the comment about a rod earlier.

Jesus, the thought of him sneaking to his car to get the rod was hot. Maybe Jake had been planning to fuck him all night—or for longer.

Jake guided the tip toward Tristan's mouth, and Tristan obediently parted his lips around the head. The taste of warm silicone was different. It was a little softer than he'd expected, but he reacted to it like sucking any cock nonetheless. The imprinted veins slid across his tongue, and the weight in his mouth gave him the same feeling he so craved.

Submission.

There was no denying it or getting around it. He was Jake's tonight, to do with as he pleased, and it thrilled him.

Jake had a plan, judging by the way he pulled back, pressing his cock for a moment against Tristan's lips and admiring the view. Then, he grabbed Tristan's thighs and hoisted him up the bed.

Tristan grunted and laughed, taking over so he could squirm all the way up the bed. "Strong."

"I don't go to the gym to look pretty." Jake followed, keeping his hand on Tristan's chest as if he weren't going to let him get away. It made Tristan's cock throb with appreciation.

"I do," Tristan snickered. "And to find pretty men to fuck me six ways from Sunday."

"What a lucky find you made, then," Jake teased. The moment Tristan reached the pillows, he crawled over him, his back straight and chin tipped up like he defied Tristan to misbehave.

Tristan ran his hands up Jake's thighs. "Lube's in the top drawer."

"I know."

"Oh. Right." Tristan laughed under his breath. They'd fucked here a few times already, and Jake was getting to know his room. And his life. It was strange how happy that made him.

Jake gave him a thoughtful look that he couldn't decipher for a moment, and then leaned over to scoop up the lube. Just the sound of the bottle snapping open had Tristan squirming with anticipation.

He caressed his shaft softly at first, and then started to jerk off.

"I could watch you play with yourself all day," Jake hummed, and then he grinned. "Maybe I should."

Tristan gasped. "With your cock right there? That's mean."

"Oh, if you insist." Jake winked and touched him with two wet fingers, running them in agonizingly slow circles around his hole at first. Then he sped up, using feather-light touches, and pressing harder, and…

The tight ring of muscle gave in as Tristan pushed against Jake's fingers, and he was inside. Jake fingered him slowly at first, moving his fingers in and out with more care than Tristan had probably ever experienced from a hookup.

But then again, as they'd danced around for weeks now, this wasn't just a hookup. *And I'm back to trying to think it through. Better to roll with the feelings.*

"What?" Jake questioned, slowing. "Does it hurt?"

Tristan realized he was smiling, too. So much that it might look like a grimace. "Not at all. You underrate my bottoming skills."

"Oh, I so hoped you had them, judging by your topping skills. It's hard to find a good vers like me." Jake thrust his fingers a little harder now, running his other hand up Tristan's chest to play with his nipples while Tristan kept jerking himself off.

"It is," Tristan agreed breathlessly. "Come on. Cock. Now."

Jake rolled a condom onto himself first, but moments later, he had the tip pressing against him.

It took Jake a moment to find his balance and angle, but the awkwardness of the first few moments didn't last. As soon as the head was in, the harder shaft filled Tristan easily, inch by inch.

Tristan was panting for breath already, his skin prickling with heat and pleasure and a touch of pain. He felt utterly vulnerable with Jake inside him.

Didn't make a damn bit of difference whether or not it was flesh and blood—it was undeniably Jake inside him, on top of him, and in charge of him.

And that thought made him grin again, giving a pleased moan. He slowed down his own hand now that Jake was inside him, wanting to last longer.

"Fuck me, baby. Show me your hot rod."

Jake snorted and smacked his chest. "That was horrible."

"It was a little funny."

"I'm in charge here, and I say it wasn't." Jake grinned, though, as he gave one thrust for emphasis. "I like fucking you, though," he added. "You don't take it too seriously. It's fun."

The pleasure crashing through him, and the need for more, erased the argument from Tristan's brain immediately. All he heard was *fucking*, and all he wanted was Jake moving inside him. "More," he whispered, and Jake obliged.

Their bodies moved in sync now, each of them somehow

understanding the other's without the awkward stops and starts, or the mismatched rhythm, or any of the hallmarks of mediocre sex that Tristan had taken for granted.

It was slow, tentative, but it felt like the beginning of something more.

With Jake, even if it wasn't perfect, it *felt* right. They were locked together in a way he didn't understand, and he didn't feel like he needed to justify or explain or even fear it.

"Does it feel good for you too?" Tristan murmured, giving him a look of concern. He didn't want to have all the fun here.

"There's bumps inside that I grind against when I go harder. I just have to get the angle right."

"Do it," Tristan whispered. "Fuck me hard, baby. Make yourself come for me."

Jake shifted, sitting a little straighter and gripping the base of his shaft with one hand, his thumb hooked into the jockstrap. His other hand stayed on Tristan's chest, idly grazing his nipple as if he'd forgotten it was there.

The feather-light touch gave him more sensations than a hard one would have, and Tristan was gasping for breath within moments.

Jake noticed. Of course he did, he always noticed these things. He started rubbing in slow circles, his finger barely contacting Tristan's skin.

"Fuck!" Tristan whimpered, pulling his knees up so Jake could fuck him deeper. Every thrust of his hips made Tristan's body tingle with pleasure.

His cock was aching for more now, but orgasm was too close. Tristan curled his fingers into the sheets to stop himself from following the temptation.

Just being under Jake would have done the job. Seeing

Jake's expressions made it ten times hotter. He loved hearing the sounds Jake made as his dick rubbed the bumps inside the bigger one.

"I love seeing you happy," Tristan whispered. He couldn't stop himself reaching up to cup Jake's cheeks, pulling him down for a kiss.

It was dirty and slow and open-mouthed as they panted against each other's lips. With every thrust, Tristan pushed up into Jake so he could go deeper and fill more of him.

"Fuck," Jake whispered, suddenly looking urgent and focused. His nails dug into Tristan's chest, making prickling sparks of painful pleasure erupt under his skin with each crescent-shaped mark. "Fuck, baby, I'm close…"

Tristan loved the pet name so much that all he could do for a second was grin at Jake. When he finally worked through that moment of bliss, he whispered, "Come on, baby. Let me feel you coming. Pound my tight little ass."

Every word of encouragement made Jake redouble his efforts, his speed hard and fast now as he gripped his own shaft tightly. Then, his back arched, his throat exposed as he threw his head back and gasped.

"Tris!"

He'd heard his name said many ways by many people, but hearing it tumbling off Jake's lips while his hips stuttered and shoved forward was like nothing else.

It was a curse and a blessing at once, and all Tristan could think was, *Fuck. I do love him.*

This wasn't supposed to happen, but following his feelings and letting his heart lead the way led him to a conclusion he couldn't avoid.

Tristan needed distraction right now.

He jerked himself off, hard and fast, as Jake slid out of

him. "Fuck… baby, that was so hot to watch," Tristan murmured.

Plenty of time to think later. He had a damn good orgasm coming to him first.

And come he did, pushing his head back into the pillows and whimpering as Jake softly ran his hands across his chest and down his arms. His whole world was Jake, and he was utterly consumed by the need he felt for him.

Jake covered Tristan's hand with his own, squeezing tightly and taking over for the last few strokes.

Jake collapsed next to him and pulled him in, wrapping his arm around his chest and pressing against his back.

Being the little spoon felt good, even if he wasn't used to feeling a still-hard shaft pressing against him. He had to remind himself that he'd already satisfied Jake.

Within minutes, they'd cleaned up, turned off the music, and turned off the lights.

Neither of them talked much as they climbed into bed together and Jake took his place behind Tristan again to hold him closer. By some unspoken agreement, they both knew they didn't need to talk.

For tonight, all they needed was to hold each other.

CHAPTER

Eleven

JAKE

"It can take some time for your menstrual cycle to resume." Dr. Lume was calm as ever, even in the face of Jake's frustration.

"But by now, I'd kind of hoped…" Jake sighed. She already knew how high his hopes were. "It could take months, couldn't it? Or years? If ever?"

"It could," she confirmed. "I'm sorry. I know that's not what you were hoping to hear."

"It's what my research told me, too," Jake said with a sigh. It bummed him out, sure, but it was also realistic. He appreciated that she didn't lie to him and string along his hopes.

"Of course, we'll want to start doing regular pregnancy tests. You could visit me on a set schedule and I can do those for you while we monitor your bloodwork and the effects of stopping testosterone."

God, for the hundredth time, Jake was glad for her. "Uh, yeah. Yeah, that's perfect. Thank you."

"How about we do the urine sample first, and I'll print the labels for your blood tests while you're busy with that?"

Jake nodded, and a minute later he was bound for the bathroom, plastic cup clenched firmly in his hand.

Only after he got there did he frown to himself. He hadn't asked if peeing through the silicone packer was okay, or if that would affect any of the tests. Now that he'd gotten used to standing to pee, sitting down was more awkward, with many more layers to worry about repositioning.

Fuck it, I'll stand.

It made aim a lot easier, at least. He left the sample in the special two-way cabinet and washed up.

By the time he was back in the room, he was alone, so he twiddled his thumbs, looked around, and tried not to worry that Tristan was stuck in the waiting room.

It was super-sweet of him to offer to drive Jake to the doctor's on the way to getting his car. Jake had figured it was an excuse to talk about them and what they were doing, but they'd both studiously managed to avoid bringing it up.

The way Tristan was acting, it was a little more than friends with benefits to him now. And frankly, Jake felt some of that same chemistry himself.

But given what he was here to do? No. When he started trying for a baby, he couldn't have a guy around to interfere with his life. The idea of kicking Tristan out of his bed and life stung, but trying to raise a kid with a friend with benefits around? Or even a boyfriend?

No way. Jake was going to raise his child the way he saw fit, and that was that.

He couldn't trust just anyone around a kid. And if he ended up infertile from hormone therapy, or just being born without cooperative eggs, adopting would be a rigorous process. They wouldn't want random guys hanging around.

However attached he was starting to grow to Tristan, he

couldn't let that dictate his actions. He had more than himself to think about.

"Ah, Jake." Dr. Lume was back, closing the door behind herself. She set down empty blood vials on the counter and wheeled closer to him.

Jake's heart was racing, and he didn't quite know why. Something about the look on her face…

He knew what she was about to say before she even said it.

Something deep inside, a gut instinct so strong it nearly overpowered reason itself, told him so.

He knew it in his very bones, and in every inch of him, and he could barely breathe.

"Jake, you're pregnant."

He nodded slowly, folding his hands between his knees and pressing them together. He could hardly feel them. Even his face felt disconnected from himself as a whirlwind of emotions hit at once.

How? When? What am I going to do?

Dr. Lume's voice broke through the fog. A touch on his shoulder, reminding him that he was right here, and he was safe here. "Deep breaths, Jake. I know it's big news. You didn't suspect?"

"Not until thirty seconds ago," Jake murmured. "I thought… but it's only been, what, six weeks?"

"Some people regain their fertility remarkably quickly."

A giggle escaped Jake. In the span of a few minutes, they'd gone from discussing how some people took a long time to get pregnant to now discovering that some people were apparently fertility machines.

And he was one of them. A relief, after worrying that he'd

find out he couldn't have his own kids, meaning years and expense added to the process.

But this was way too soon.

Dr. Lume squeezed his arm again. "Keep breathing, Jake. How are you feeling?"

"In shock," Jake admitted, but at least the initial adrenaline surge was starting to fade. "I didn't expect it to be this fast. And I haven't... we never had unprotected sex... oh, man. How far am I? Is it within, like, the last month? It would have to be. It's only been..." he trailed off, rubbing his face.

He'd always heard—from pharmacists, therapists, Dr. Lume herself—that testosterone alone wasn't good birth control. But he'd never had a scare like this before. He'd never even considered it possible.

Then again, he'd never been off testosterone since starting it, and he'd never had sex before he started testosterone. But the condoms?

"Well, we can't count from the date of your last missed period. We can tell by ultrasound when you're about ten to fourteen weeks along. Do you have an idea of a conception date, somewhere between two and four weeks ago?"

Jake giggled again, the stress and shock going to his head. "Any day. Most days. We've been... I mean, I've been seeing one guy a lot. But we used condoms. But I wasn't really thinking about changing them if it was a marathon. I've gotten so used to thinking it wouldn't happen..."

She gave him a sympathetic smile. "They do fail. It looks like you're at the center of the perfect storm: fertility and a failed condom."

Jake laughed. "There were plenty of chances for it to fail."

"Is this the guy in the waiting room?"

Jake blushed, and it felt like it was from head to toe. "Um. Yeah."

"If you need to discuss family planning matters with him, you're welcome to bring him in."

"No. No way!" Jake sat up straight, his heart thudding. "I don't want him involved. He'll think—oh, God. What if he thinks it was deliberate? I didn't want to be parenting while dating. I was trying not to get involved, and now... oh, crap."

"Everything that happens is your decision," Dr. Lume told him, and he drew strength from her steadiness. "I'll do tests first while we talk about it, and we can make sure there won't be an effect on the baby from your current hormone levels, plus the usual prenatal tests."

Prenatal. This was huge. This was... life-changing.

If he carried this pregnancy to term, he was going to be a... mother? Father? He hadn't even decided which word he wanted to use! And he was going to be a parent, in less than a year, to a newborn who was relying on him for everything.

Jake buried his face in his hands and took a few more deep breaths to calm himself down.

I'll find a way, he thought. *I always do.*

From the moment he'd realized who he was, he'd drawn on inner strength he hadn't even known he had. This was no different. This involved other people now, but it was still his body, and his choices, and his life. And he was going to set this baby up with the life they deserved.

If that meant lying awake and panicking, he could do that later. For now, he needed tests and information and help, and Dr. Lume was here.

He'd worry about what to tell Tristan when he got to the waiting room.

"Okay. I'm ready for the tests."

CHAPTER

Twelve

TRISTAN

The moment Jake walked out of the exam room, something looked different about him.

Tristan couldn't put a name to it, exactly, and he wasn't going to pry right here in the waiting room. He just smiled and offered his hand to Jake, who took it. "Ready to go?"

"Yep." Jake was unusually quiet in his response as he nodded to the door.

Tristan just hoped it wasn't bad news. Suddenly, his whole heart had become tied up in this man—far more than he'd expected it to be.

Ever since last night, the same argument had been going around and around his head.

I can't possibly be in love yet! But I am. There's something that pulled me to him right away. Hell, it did years ago. Why is that so hard to believe?

If he were really honest, it was because he knew how easy it was to act. Actors lied professionally; plenty of actors he knew lied in their personal lives, too. Hell, so did he.

How was he supposed to trust himself when it could just

be… well, desperation, or lust, or platonic attraction to a guy who could hold a conversation?

He hadn't figured anything out, and bringing it up before he did seemed stupid. He had to know what he wanted before he asked Jake about it.

"Everything okay?" he asked once he was in the car.

Jake swallowed hard. "Can we get McFlurries and talk?" His voice wavered, and he wouldn't look at Tristan.

He's dumping me. Tristan swallowed hard and nodded, trying to search his suddenly-blank mind for the nearest McDonald's. "Um. Sure. It's… I think there's one nearby…"

"Two blocks away," Jake pointed.

"A familiar spot?" Tristan joked, but Jake didn't respond. He just gazed out the window, a frown line between his brows.

Okay, this definitely wasn't good news.

The drive was quick, which was a small mercy given that it was completely silent. Even if they hadn't argued, weirdly enough, it felt like they had.

"Drive-through or eat in?"

Jake squinted out the car window into the McDonald's and shaded his eyes. When Tristan followed his gaze, he saw one of those play centers and a bunch of stressed-looking moms.

"Drive-through. We can find a spot to park and eat. Better than being surrounded by…" Jake trailed off.

Tristan grinned. "Screaming kids?"

"Yeah." Jake's voice was a whisper. He was back to staring out the window like he'd barely heard the question.

"What kind of flurry?" Tristan asked, nudging Jake gently. At least Jake didn't pull away, just offered him a distracted smile.

"Oreo, please."

"Sure thing." He had to bite his tongue before he added *baby*. If he was about to get dumped, he was going to do it when he already had the ice cream in his hand.

After they got their ice creams, Tristan found a parking lot nearby. It was next to what passed for a garden in this part of LA: mostly a strip of gravel and a few scrawny palm trees, and a bunch of flowering bushes.

That was about as romantic as this was going to get.

He shut off the engine and popped the lid off, then prepared to dig his spoon in. "Cheers!" He raised the spoon like a shot glass.

"I'm pregnant."

Tristan blinked a few times. He couldn't possibly have heard that right, could he? Was Jake joking? But this wasn't exactly joking material, and he said it so quietly... like he was afraid of the response.

After a few seconds, Tristan's brain engaged. *He means with my kid.* "Oh, my God."

"I'm sorry this isn't a better time or place to tell you... I wasn't going to, but the doctor said I should. I realized it was only right you knew, even if it's mine to deal with. It wasn't deliberate. I didn't know I *could* get pregnant yet."

Jake was looking at him now, his gaze wide. It was the closest to fear he'd seen on the face of this man, and Tristan wanted to wrap his arms around him and take the feeling away.

"But we were... we used condoms." Tristan realized he was still holding the spoon in the air, and his other hand was going numb. He looked like the goddamn Statue of Liberty. He quickly balanced the flurry on his knee and stuck the spoon in, then reached out to touch Jake's knee.

"I know. That's what I told her." Jake's lips quirked up into a little smile. "But it happens. I had a friend in high school who had sex twice with her first boyfriend, and they used condoms. They didn't notice them breaking, but she got pregnant. I'm just so used to thinking testosterone would stop it…"

"Right," Tristan murmured. Jake had been wanting a kid, so this wasn't the worst thing ever, right? "It's for sure mine?"

"You're the only guy I've wanted…" Jake cut himself off as if he hadn't meant to say that. "That I've fucked. In a couple months. Since stopping T."

That was almost as big a piece of news as the pregnancy. *There's hope for an* us, *even if everything will change now.* Tristan bit his tongue, and then started working on the McFlurry as he tried to sort out his feelings. "Is this a craving?"

"Huh?" Jake looked at the ice cream, and then over at Tristan. He laughed abruptly and shook his head. "No. But since I can't drown my thoughts in wine, ice cream will have to do."

Duh. So many tiny things that Tristan hadn't even thought of. He'd never even considered he'd ever get anyone pregnant.

As far as most gay men were concerned, it was a huge relief—something not to worry about. He'd joined in that sentiment, all the while feeling the itch somewhere deep in his gut. The instinct to have a child of his own.

And now…

"Fuck. I should have asked first," Tristan murmured, looking over. "Are you keeping it? Do you know yet?" There was probably a more sensitive way to ask that, but he was too addled by shock to think clearly.

"Yeah. I am. If all goes well." Jake gripped his Flurry so tightly the lid popped off, and he had to chuckle as he retrieved it. "I mean, I was planning on it taking a while to even be able to get pregnant. I was gonna—well, you already know. Find a stable job, get a better place to live… this wasn't the right time."

Tristan's mouth went dry as the future came crashing in on him. This was a change to everything he'd been thinking.

If he was going to support them, he couldn't just walk away from acting and spend years dicking around in school finding something else to do.

He was going to take that movie role, if they offered it to him.

"I'm not an expert," he murmured, "but I've heard there's never a right time to have a baby."

Jake laughed. "There are definitely better times. But at least this is what I wanted. It's just… so soon. I was going to read books, and talk to people, and find support networks…" he trailed off. His voice was suddenly hoarse.

Tristan touched his arm again. "My friends Kyle and Nic might know people. And they'll support you. They have a kid."

"Oh. They do?" Jake brightened up a little. "I know a few people with them, but… mostly straight people. Anyway, I think I'll… I'll head home now. I don't want to think about it. I need a nap, and some time to figure all this out."

"I don't blame you," Tristan exclaimed. He hadn't even really figured out how he felt, either. "Of course."

"Let's head back to my car," Jake told him. He seemed more like himself than before, so even if he was brushing Tristan off now, Tristan felt better about leaving him on his own to come to terms with it.

He nodded and slid the flurry into his cup holder as he started up the car. "Of course."

Tristan's heart raced as he counted down the minutes to the parking lot. Now seemed like the least sensitive time to ask what that meant for the two of them.

Next time he saw Jake, he'd ask.

As they pulled into the restaurant parking lot and he found a spot by Jake's car, Tristan asked, "Are you free next week?"

Jake shrugged as he finished his ice cream and popped the lid back on. "I don't know. I didn't think to check the schedule before I left yesterday, sorry."

Tristan laughed. "No, I think that was my fault."

"And a good kind of blame to take." Jake smirked, clearly remembering their incredible sex last night.

Tristan tried not to chuckle. Having Jake inside him, and finding out the very next day that Jake was pregnant, was a weird kind of mindfuck.

"What?"

"It's just... I never expected any of this. Babies, and seeing you a lot, and... you know. Big life changes."

Jake gave him a smile as he unbuckled. "Yeah. Thanks for taking it well. I wasn't sure how you were going to react."

"Yeah, I bet." Tristan laughed. "Finding out you're pregnant... I mean. That's definitely not what I've ever expected. Fucking girls has its risks. But getting a guy pregnant? That's not normal."

The moment he said it, he knew he'd made a mistake. He'd been on the receiving end of *not normal* too many times not to know. And he hadn't meant it that way, but it was undoubtedly a slap in the face to hear.

Jake's expression closed off, and he opened the car door to climb out.

"Shit," Tristan breathed out, fumbling to unbuckle and climb out. That put his car between them, though, and those few feet might as well have been a mile. "Honey, I didn't…"

"Don't call me that." Jake's voice was sharp, and it stung.

Tristan swallowed hard and curled his hands into fists. "Sorry. Jake. I didn't mean it that way."

"I know what you meant." Jake still wasn't looking at him as he dug out his car keys and opened the car door. "It's fine."

His entire body language screamed *not fine*, but Tristan didn't feel like he had any right to stop him leaving and explain himself. Hell, they were just friends and fuck-buddies. And he might have fucked up both of those things in one breath.

Tristan felt even worse that it hadn't just been the wrong word. Saying *I meant uncommon* wouldn't change anything.

It was still the same idea. Nobody wanted to feel like the rare freak in the crowd—a circus sideshow. Well, Jake probably didn't, at least.

And he was facing down months of getting that treatment from the rest of the world, in order to do something that most of the world took for granted.

"No, it isn't," Tristan said quietly. "Look, call me when you want to talk, okay?"

At last, Jake looked at him. He said nothing, but he gave him a small, sad smile.

Tristan's heart jolted. *Fuck. He wants to ditch me, doesn't he?* He wasn't going to play the *biological rights* card just to make Jake stay, though. That would be disrespectful as hell after what he'd just said.

"I mean it," Tristan added sternly. "Whether or not you

want help, or financial support, or anything. I care about you as a friend. No matter my role, I want to be there."

Jake held his gaze for a few long moments, and finally relented. He let out his breath and nodded. "We'll talk," he promised.

Relief coursed through Tristan, making his shoulders sag as he leaned on the hood of his car. For a second there, he'd been terrified that he'd just lost him.

It wasn't like a fuck-buddy getting busy with life and moving on without him. Tristan would have taken it far harder than that, and not just because of the baby who was now involved. He'd already been thinking about bringing it up, but too scared to do so.

Now they really needed to talk—but first, Jake needed space.

"Call me," he said again. "Take care, Jake."

Jake drew a breath and let it out, then nodded. "Talk to you soon."

Tristan raised a hand when Jake drove away, then leaned on his car hood.

Thankfully, it wasn't scorching hot. He didn't need a mirror of the burning embarrassment that coursed through him.

Tristan didn't know a lot about trans issues, but he knew what he'd seen in headlines. Every so often, a "pregnant man" news story would pop up, online or in a newspaper.

The rest of the world was about to tell Jake that he was wrong, or bad, or not really a man, or a pervert, or all kinds of horrible things… just for wanting something that so many people wanted. To have a family.

Adding to that burden made Tristan feel the worst he'd felt about himself in a long time.

From now on, he was going to do his damn best to make Jake feel normal, yet special, like anyone else who was pregnant. However possible, Tristan wanted to care for and about Jake.

All he could do now was pray that Jake gave him the chance to figure out how.

CHAPTER

Thirteen

JAKE

It was the wrong five o'clock to wake up. Far from his usual early mornings, the sun was creeping toward the horizon when Jake finally made himself get out of bed.

A short nap had turned into a longer one. He'd obviously been tired enough to need the rest, and going to work was the last thing he wanted to do… but he needed the job, too. Rent didn't pay itself.

"Get up and at 'em," Jake told himself as he pushed the flimsy closet door open.

Half his closet was plain clothes: black trousers and white button-down shirts for the restaurant, and more shades of black for his set work. He'd gotten into the color scheme in high school theater club, and he'd stuck with it. It made getting dressed easy.

Oh, God. All his clothes fit him well, which meant in a few months' time, they wouldn't.

He took a few deep breaths and sat on the bed again, staring at the open closet. There were a hundred details—a thousand, maybe—that he hadn't sorted out yet.

Jake had expected to have so much more time to think it through. To carefully plan and set it up. And now he was plunging headlong into this, without a second to waste.

He couldn't be more than two weeks along, but that meant just thirty-eight weeks to go. It was a number that seemed both forever away and way too soon.

He'd been in California for six years. Thirty-eight weeks? That was nothing.

It was still early. Way too early to count on anything. Of all the things Dr. Lume had told him, that sank in, at least.

The first trimester, anything might go wrong. If anything did, it was likely in the next few months. His bloodwork results had yet to come back. This was so soon after stopping testosterone that the hormone balance could be all wrong.

She'd done all she could to caution him against getting excited, and planning his life around the coming new one, but... a kind of certainty had settled in him now.

He was going to be a parent. Until and unless anything went wrong later, he *was* going to plan his life as best he could.

And that meant getting to work, swallowing the irritability and low energy and moodiness, serving customers the best he could to get as many tips as he could, and worrying about everything else later. Not just for his own sake now.

This baby was his responsibility, and his alone. The only other person involved was... well, Tristan.

"God," Jake mumbled under his breath. "Get ready for work, loser." If he didn't get out the door in twenty minutes, traffic might make him late. That was the last thing he needed.

As Jake dressed and tidied up his hair, he couldn't help

but think of Tristan. He felt bad for having shut him out this morning. But hearing that word—*normal*—had made it all hit home for him.

This *wasn't* normal. This was far from it. He had Dr. Lume on his side, but he was going to need to deal with obstetricians, and nurses, and doctors, and God only knew who else.

And he was probably going to be the only pregnant guy anybody knew.

He was utterly alone, as he had been for so damn long. And for once, it didn't feel good. He didn't want to be alone, and admitting that to himself hurt.

Jake's hands shook as he buttoned up his shirt and shoved the tails in his trousers. He slipped a thumb in his waistband to check the button, drawing a deep breath as his fingers brushed the outline of his silicone cock. He shifted his three layers of waistbands so it all sat right on his hips, and then grabbed his tie.

A few minutes in the bathroom and he looked like he hadn't been napping the afternoon away. He was still tired out, but when had that ever stopped him from being a super-star—on set, on the restaurant floor, or wherever else he needed to be?

When there was a job to be done, he rose to the occasion. And he was about to get the biggest job title of his life.

There was no reason he couldn't do it—alone or not.

But why should I be alone?

That was a thought to contemplate after work, not before.

"So, how were things last night?" Amanda greeted him with a grin as she printed a check from the point-of-sale system.

Jake blew out a little sigh and laughed, not sure where to begin explaining.

She eyed him closely before shaking her head. "Sounds like a long story. Drinks tonight after our shift?"

She hadn't invited him out before. Jake smiled, recognizing this as an attempt at friendship. First Kyle and his friendship group, and now Amanda? How was he suddenly making all these friends, after years of getting by?

Maybe he'd finally opened his eyes to the people around him.

"Sure. Drinks tonight." Jake neglected to mention that drinking was going to be off the table for a long time to come. A lot of tonic water lay ahead of him.

"Great. Move, I need a pen."

The abruptness was just par for the course here, and it meant they were comfortable together. Jake grinned as he leaned back, grabbed one, and handed it over.

"Thanks."

She strode off for her table and he looked around at the place to get his bearings. Then, he headed back to the kitchen to check with Milo for today's specialties and menu changes.

"That was some fellow you brought in yesterday," Milo commented as he sprinkled cheese on a bubbling-hot pan of macaroni.

Jake sighed and pressed his palm against his forehead. "Is my dating life that bad that that's all everyone has to talk about?"

"Well..." Milo pretended to think. "Yes."

"Rude," Jake teased, propping his chin on his fist. "Besides, I don't know if I'll keep him around."

Milo spluttered. "I might be a confirmed bachelor, but even I'm gonna say that's a dumbass move. The man's got eyes for you, and you for him. What's in the way?"

"Lifestyle," Jake said, trying to evade the questioning. He had to get to the front door and seat another party who had just arrived. Dinner service was about to begin, and he didn't want to leave *that* conversation hanging.

Milo let it go. It was the nature of this kind of work—snippets of conversation between covers, and fragile friendships as they learned to dodge and weave around each other, keeping the chaos behind the scenes so diners had a pleasant experience.

The better you were at bowing and scraping, the more you'd earn. This place at least paid minimum wage, in addition to the healthcare benefits.

Oh, God. Would his insurance cover the pregnancy costs? Now that he was named as male on his policy, he already had to fight for things like pap smears to be covered. They might try anything to avoid paying those costs.

Deep breath, and deal with it later.

"Hi, welcome!" he greeted, pasting the sunniest smile he could manage onto his face as he led the group to their table.

He had to have faith that everything would work out, and pour whatever he could into the only things he could control. Right now, all he could control was how hard he worked, so he was going to be the best he could at his job.

Later, he'd figure out whether he wanted to call Tristan... or if he could stand not to.

The shift passed mercifully quickly, the pace picking up minutes later when several large groups arrived.

By the end of the night, his feet hurt, his face hurt from forcing so many smiles, and his wallet was thicker than it had been in a while.

"You killed it tonight," Amanda told him as she counted up the register. It was just the two of them left in the place now to close it out. "You've got your mojo back."

"Back?"

"Oh." Amanda gave a sheepish smile. "You just seemed like… not yourself. And the tips…"

Jake instantly understood. They pooled tips, so anyone getting low tips affected everyone else. "Shit. Sorry," he mumbled.

"No, it's all right. We've all got those bad days, or weeks."

"Or six weeks now," Jake said, half-smiling. "My hormones have been nuts."

"Ohhh." Amanda nodded. "Like PMS? Does that happen a lot?"

"Worse than PMS was for me, but I used to be lucky that way." Jake leaned on the counter and tidied it up, out of sheer habit. He couldn't keep his hands idle for long. "Now I'm moody as hell."

"When I lived at home with my mom, it's a wonder we didn't throttle each other that time of the month," Amanda laughed. "Are you getting better now?"

"No," Jake admitted, rubbing his face. "But that's a… that's a long story."

Worse than the idea of telling anyone he was pregnant—and he knew how risky that was in a job like this—was the idea of having to tell them if anything went wrong. He'd promised to himself he wouldn't let on until the first trimester was safely over.

He'd quietly go about setting his own life to rights, and keep it to himself as he figured out how to make this work.

Jake caught himself with his hand on his stomach. God, he was going to have to get out of that habit before he started to grow.

He headed for the staff room to grab his phone and change into street shoes. A few minutes later, after depositing the cash into the safe, Amanda joined him by the front door.

"Drinks around the corner? Then we can leave our cars here."

"I won't drink anyway," Jake told her. "But somewhere close is good. I don't want to be up until all hours. I'm an old man."

Amanda gasped. "Fuck off. You aren't."

"I feel like it."

"If you're old, I'm decrepit. Thirty-four next week, thanks very much!"

Jake stared. "Really?" It was the polite thing to say, but it was also true. She didn't look it.

Amanda softened and grinned. "If I didn't know how gay you were, I'd say you were flirting. Well done, darling. Your first drink's on me."

"I wasn't—I mean, it's true." Jake laughed as they walked around two empty strip mall buildings to the bar. It was still vibrant and bustling at this time of night, even if nowhere else around it was. "This a good place?"

"You haven't been? Dude, how long have you been working here and I haven't invited you out for drinks? Oh, my God." Amanda covered her face. "You must have thought I hated you!"

Jake shook his head. "No, no. I took off ASAP for months. You never had the chance."

"Well, we're fixing that now," Amanda told him as they headed in and up to the bar. "Sure you don't want a drink?"

"Yep. I don't drink," Jake said firmly. The sooner he established that peer pressure wouldn't work, the better.

Luckily, Amanda took it just fine. "Sure. What can I get you instead?"

He settled for a Coke while she got a rum and Coke, and they found a table nearby. This was such a different place from his usual haunts when he did go out—more women, way more straight guys, and a vibe he wasn't altogether comfortable with.

Still, as Amanda peppered him with questions that he did his best to dodge and return to her, Jake relaxed.

He was finally making friends and establishing a real life for himself, not just counting down the hours between shifts.

But it wasn't like hanging out with Tristan. Tristan meant something more to him, and like it or not, he was going to have to come to terms with that.

Tomorrow wasn't going to be the day in bed he'd promised himself. He just hoped it would be even better. The way they'd left off, he wasn't sure.

But Jake owed it to himself to talk to Tristan, not just run away from anything potentially good in his life because the timing wasn't right.

Maybe Tristan was right, and the timing was never right for a baby. That applied to men, too. And he was growing increasingly certain that what he wanted was Tristan.

Jake had never let timing stop him from getting what he wanted before.

Why start now?

"I WANT TO WORK. I DON'T CARE IF IT'S FOR STUPID commercials. If I'm not getting work, I'm basically just waiting to be slowly pushed out of Hollywood."

Tristan paced back and forth in Bobby's office, his hands folded behind his back as he stepped around the piles of paperwork. They seemed to build up whenever Bobby's personal assistant took one of those rare days off.

He worked best spreading casting calls and photos and that kind of shit on the floor. Like an actor's process, Tristan didn't question it.

"You've got a fire under your ass all of a sudden," Bobby told him. "I thought you were done with demeaning roles. We were moving your brand toward *leading man*. Because you wanted to play straight."

Tristan snorted quietly and shook his head. "It's not worth my career over. Either I work or I find a new industry. I appreciate being able to pay my bills—I mean, I make more than the average underemployed actor in town. I get that. But I'm never going to break out at this rate."

"No," Bobby agreed, to his surprise. "You want the honest truth, Tristan?"

"Please." Tristan turned on his feel to face the man, staring across his cluttered desk at him.

He'd trusted Bobby with his career for the last three years, and Bobby hadn't let him down. He'd managed to find Tristan enough work. Not *great* work, but he wouldn't be living in the place he did without Bobby's help—and the help of the investment advisor Bobby had pointed him toward. When Bobby spoke, Tristan listened.

"You need to either commit to working your ass off and going to everything I send you, and you trust me to steer you right, or you find another career where you're self-directed."

Tristan blinked a few times. "Self-directed?"

"You take the reins a lot. And I respect that. It means you care. But it also means I can't send you to jobs without you side-eyeing me," Bobby said.

Tristan choked back his defensiveness and breathed for a few moments, making himself sit with the criticism. Something about it must have been true, because it stung to hear put so plainly. Finally, he nodded. "Okay. Yeah. I do turn down some work. And I was pissed off about the commercials."

"They wanted someone to play camp."

"I'm not camp." It wasn't a bad thing, but to someone who'd worked hard not to be seen that way, it was scary to think people might see what he tried to keep hidden.

"You're not," Bobby agreed, not rising to Tristan's defensiveness. "I don't think you should be afraid of playing around with the way you're seen, though. You're a goddamn actor. The less like yourself you are, the better a job you're doing. That doesn't translate to real life. Don't screw up your life in the pursuit of a career."

Tristan's cheeks burned. That hit home even more than Bobby's last statement. All he let himself say was, "Oh."

"The more you hide yourself, the more you *have* to hide, the less energy you have to put into putting masks on top of your masks."

"Are you saying I should come out?"

That kind of aligned with his own desires right now, for the first time. He'd so fiercely resisted any hint of gayness in his filmography.

But if he was thinking about ditching the industry... why not? If he got typecast, he could just burn it all down and walk away.

"No," Bobby said quickly. "I wouldn't just tell anyone to come out. It's not a nice industry. But if I could use that information behind the scenes... feed it to the right people..."

Tristan dropped into the chair opposite Bobby, bracing his elbows on his knees and leaning forward to press his head into his hands. "No."

"You're a big enough name that you can coast by for a bit. People will deliberately turn a blind eye. But not so big a name you can get late-night talk show spots by coming out live, you know? It's a hard place to be," Bobby told him. "I just want you to get the credit, not play the whole damn role 24/7."

"Fine. I'll audition for the gay part. I want to."

Bobby raised his brow. "That's a change of heart, but I'm glad to hear it. He asked specifically for you. You've got a great chance. But can I ask something? If you're not coming out, why?"

Tristan shrugged. He didn't have a lot of secrets from Bobby. So far, he hadn't told him about Jake, but that was about it. Because there was nothing *to* tell yet. "I'm tired of cobbling together work," Tristan said.

Bobby eyed him for a few long moments and then folded his arms. He said nothing.

Tristan had studied the human psyche. He knew how uncomfortable people got with silence. How you could use that to your advantage, make other people fill the silence with the answers you wanted. He knew all of that, but he couldn't stop himself.

"Okay, and I need money."

"Why?" Bobby challenged. He could see the thoughts written on Bobby's face as plain as day: *Drugs? Fast cars? What does Tristan need?*

"Why do you need to know?"

"Because I need to know that you're in this to win this. Like you did to get to this point. You wanted me to get more picky, so I did. But you're not auditioning anymore."

Tristan didn't miss those days. Day after day being shot down, or outright blanked. Never hearing back, wondering if he was really that shitty.

It was hell on the ego, and if he were truthful with himself, it wasn't branding making him choosier. It was not being able to handle that rejection, over and over again.

Oh, fuck. It was just like Grindr. They had the same effect —of grinding down his ego, until he wondered whether he was good enough for anyone at all.

"I can do it," Tristan said quietly. "I won't tell you why, but the reason is compelling enough to make me work my ass off. And any day I don't have an audition, I'm going to work on something else. I don't know what yet," he interrupted before Bobby could ask, "but something. Bartending? My own business? I don't care. But I need steady work."

Bobby folded his hands across his stomach and leaned back as Tristan prayed he didn't ask more questions. Finally, Bobby nodded. "Have it your way. If you've done something stupid, don't let me find out from the gossip blogs."

"I haven't," Tristan assured him, smiling. "I might come out about it. We'll see. You'll be the first to know."

"Okay. I gotta give this guy a call. Hang onto your phone, Tristan. And be ready for an audition anytime. And think about letting me tell people. There are whisper networks. You end up with the right casting director, he could get you a groundbreaking part."

"I'm keeping my private life private. I'm not fighting it if it comes out, but I'm not gonna try to be a poster boy." Tristan stood up and leaned in to shake hands. "I'll play my part."

"And I mine." Bobby shook hands firmly. "Let's do this."

Tristan was still buzzing from the meeting by the time he got to his favorite coffee shop, not far from Plus. He planned to pick up half a dozen coffees and bring them to the charity. The guys there loved it when he did.

He hung out here while waiting for callbacks, memorizing sides, or if they sent him home early from a job. It was a friendly place with familiar baristas, good wifi, and nice artwork.

But now that he was more familiar with the Plus crowd, and less concerned with being outed, he felt less shy about going there to hang out, so he brought them coffee and got social interaction. Win all around.

God, he loved that smell. Coffee meant early mornings

and late nights on set. To him, it smelled like work. It was a prayer for more, like a good-luck charm.

Speaking of *more…*

He checked his phone, half-expecting nothing but stupid new emails. But there was a text waiting for him from Jake, and it made his heart leap.

Are you free today?

For Jake? Fuck, yeah. He sent a quick text back.

I am now :) About to bring coffee to Plus.

He had his answer within moments.

Can I meet you there?

Of course! See you soon?

On my way now.

Tristan pocketed his phone and carried the carefully-stacked trays out to the car again. This last part of the drive was always the trickiest, and he drove gently to keep the coffee from sloshing out of the sealed cups and onto his seats.

He and his seats made it, and soon he was juggling his way through the front entrance, waiting to be let into the building.

Tristan hadn't seen the guys since that night in the club, which meant he probably had about ten minutes to explain his relationship with Jake and ask them not to scare him off. No big deal, right?

"Hey! You come bearing coffee!" Kyle beamed as he pushed open the door and held it.

"I don't know how long I'll stay. Jake's on the way. He said he'd meet me here, and I… I need to talk to him. I've been a dumbass." The words spilled out of Tristan before he could stop them, and he stared at Kyle, as much in surprise at himself as in need of an answer—any answer. "I don't know how to make him feel at ease, as a trans guy, and I don't want to fuck it up again. Can you help?"

Kyle stared for a few moments, and then took the coffee from him. "Come on, honey. Let me grab these. How long do we have to troubleshoot?"

"Ten minutes?"

Kyle nodded. "Let's go."

Once they were upstairs, Kyle distributed coffees and steered Tristan straight to a meeting room, then closed the door behind them and grabbed a chair beside Tristan. "Spill."

"I like him. He just wants to be fuck-buddies. I was thinking about quitting acting so I don't have to be so... so closeted. And..." Tristan trailed off, then sighed. The rest of the story wasn't his to tell. He couldn't out Jake's pregnancy, could he? "Basically, I think he'll need support, and I want to be the one to support him, but he'll never accept it. We're not even dating yet. I don't know what we're doing."

Kyle nodded. "So, it's complicated?"

"Yeah. And I said something dumb that made him feel..." Tristan trailed off, glancing down. "Well, not normal, I think. I used that exact word. What was I thinking? I meant *uncommon*, but even that just makes him remember who he is, and maybe not in a nice way..."

Kyle reached out to hold Tristan's hand and squeezed. "Hey. Deep breath."

Tristan hadn't even noticed himself getting dizzy. He obediently breathed in and out, then covered his face. "I'm being such an idiot, and I don't even think he loves me."

The words hung in the air between them for a few moments, but there was no taking them back.

"Do you want me to call Zeph?" Kyle asked softly. "I can help you, as the partner of a trans guy who's spent a bit of time thinking about how not to hurt him. But if you want your best friend here…"

Tristan shook his head. "I haven't told him anything about this either."

"Well, no more keeping this to yourself," Kyle told him sternly. "Not when we're here to help. Okay?"

"Yeah." Tristan offered a little smile. "Thanks. I know this is all out of the blue."

"You're brightening up a boring Tuesday. I appreciate it." Kyle smiled, and Tristan felt comfortable with him. "So he knows you didn't mean to be a dick."

"Yeah, he—"

"It wasn't a question." Kyle smiled kindly. "I'm telling you, he knows. We all know when someone was trying to hurt us or wasn't. Trans people especially are tuned into that. So don't fall over yourself to try to prove that you didn't mean to. Just apologize once and move on."

Tristan nodded slowly. It lined up with what he'd heard Nic say before. "And what if he doesn't forgive me?"

"What the hell did you say? Just that you don't normally do something?"

"Something like that."

Kyle smiled. "You weren't demeaning him deliberately. I know that much about you. He'll forgive you, as long as you talk it out. And try to do better next time. People aren't perfect, and he's got enough experience under his belt to be able to withstand a few unintentional ouchies."

"I hope so," Tristan murmured.

"And I think you need to think about how attached you are to him. If you're here panicking because he might stop talking to you… it's not just fuck-buddies."

Tristan's feelings were shutting down his logical side. All

he could do was trust that Kyle was right. "I know. I already know I love him, and I know it's stupid and too soon and…"

"Not too soon," Kyle interrupted gently. "People can look at each other and just *know*. You still have to do a hell of a lot of work to make it become a relationship and survive long-term, but you can feel the initial click right away. As for stupid… love isn't stupid," he added, his voice suddenly fierce. "Don't believe that for a second."

"I don't," Tristan admitted. "I just think *I* am."

Kyle snorted. "Not from everything Zeph's said, so don't you dare put yourself down like that. Look: he's coming here to talk to you. He wants to give you a chance. He's not just texting you and running."

The faint sound of a phone ringing told them both that they had company.

"You've got this," Kyle added with a smile, squeezing his hand again before he stood up.

That phone meant Jake was here, and Tristan just wanted to sweep him off his feet and make him feel exactly as precious as he deserved.

As long as he got the chance.

CHAPTER

Fifteen

JAKE

Jake couldn't stay with Tristan. Not after the kid was born, anyway. But the thought of not seeing him anymore? It made his heart ache in his chest, in a way it hadn't done since his last breakup.

Fuck, this wasn't even a breakup. It wasn't a relationship. They'd talked and talked about maybe prolonging it, or maybe feeling things for each other, but neither of them had ever suggested making it official.

And now with a baby in the mix… he couldn't let Tristan stay with him out of some sense of honor. Jake wasn't something to be looked after, like he couldn't make his own damn way in the world.

"Hey," he greeted Kyle when he came to meet him at the door, just like before.

"Hi, darling!" Kyle greeted and air-kissed his cheeks. "Come on in. How have you been?"

Jake chuckled. "A lot's happened," he admitted.

"Good things, I hope." Kyle gave him an anxious look, and Jake had to admit it felt nice to be cared about.

"Yeah. Yeah, good things. Just big things. Is, uh… is Tristan here?"

"He is. He's waiting to talk to you," Kyle said with a meaningful glance his way that Jake couldn't quite decipher.

"Oh. Good." How much had Tristan told him? "Um, but first… thank you for those email addresses you gave me." He'd emailed the doula Kyle had pointed him to last night, and they had already responded with information and some internet links to read.

It felt a little less overwhelming not to be going this completely alone.

Kyle beamed. "Of course! Anything I can help with, you know I will."

"You might be able to. We'll see how it goes with the people you connected me to," Jake said as he walked through the final set of doors into the Plus office.

He immediately spotted Tristan. God, it was like every time he walked into the room, a part of his brain did a subconscious *Tristan check*. If Tristan was there, he was the first thing Jake noticed, and the center of his attention.

Jake had once blamed that magnetic movie star attraction, but it was more than that. It was something personal now, attuned straight to the real Tristan, not the on-screen personality. To all his laughter and teasing, and his quiet moments of vulnerability, and how goddamn sexy he was whether on the top or the bottom.

And then there was the way he relaxed when he walked into a room and Tristan was there. It wasn't like his stresses were suddenly gone, but it felt like…

Well, like he wasn't so alone.

The way Tristan lit up in response made him blush.

Whatever this was felt so damn obvious to bystanders. No way could anyone fail to notice.

"Hey," Tristan greeted as he strode over to the door. Then he seemed to hesitate, as if unsure what attention Jake would welcome in public. He reached out a hand to take Jake's, a little hesitantly.

Jake let him—he more than let him, in fact. He squeezed tightly in return, trying to convey an ounce of the complicated feelings that hit him. Because no matter what his logical brain told him about cutting ties, his heart wasn't having any of it.

"Shall we go get McFlurries?"

That, at least, made Jake smile. "I think I'm good for those. I'd kill for some fries, though."

"Fries it is." Tristan raised a hand and waved at the rest of the office, and so did Jake. Leaving on Tristan's arm, so soon after getting here... well, he felt kind of like his boyfriend.

They didn't say anything at first as they headed through the hallways together, and back out to the parking lot. But neither of them moved to drop hands, either.

Jake burst out, "We should talk."

At the same moment, Tristan had started to say, "So, I was thinking..."

They both broke off and looked at each other, their fingers wedged tightly between one another's, as if afraid to let go.

"Yeah. Yeah, we should talk. McDonald's fries and the park? I know one nearby," Tristan suggested.

"An actual park? Is it the size of a stamp?"

Tristan laughed, and that gorgeous sound made Jake instinctively relax, like it was fine-tuned to sweep away his cares. At least, whatever the hell they said, Tristan didn't hate him for not getting in touch yesterday. "Yeah," Tristan said. "You wanna drive or me?"

"I'll take a turn," Jake told him. At least this way, he was in control.

But he wasn't going to run away this time. He couldn't just keep escaping anything he didn't like to think about. It wasn't going to serve him well in his new life, and if Tristan was going to be part of it... he had to stop it.

By the time they sat on the one unoccupied bench in the little green space, each of them clutching a brown paper bag filled with fries rapidly losing their heat and firmness, they were joking about Star Wars and something Jake had heard on the radio.

The moment they sat, though, their promise to talk seemed to come crashing in on them both at the same time.

"You first," Jake said. It was the least he could do to offer Tristan a chance to talk, after he'd all but stormed away a few days ago. He opened his bag and grabbed a few fries at a time.

God, the grease was exactly what he'd needed right now. Either this was the beginning of his pregnancy cravings, or he'd been craving junk food to make up for the stress of thinking—or trying not to think—about what he and Tristan were going to do.

Tristan drew a breath and looked at him, not even opening his bag yet. "Okay. I'm sorry I said this whole situation isn't normal, first off. I hope you know I didn't mean to hurt you. I don't think being out of the ordinary is a bad thing, but I get that you probably don't need the... unusualness... rubbed in your face right now."

A quick breath rushed out of Jake's lungs. That pretty much summed up everything he'd had to say. "Thank you," he murmured. He bit his lip for a moment, and then licked the salt off his fingers so he could squeeze Tristan's knee. "I'm really grateful that you're putting yourself in my shoes when this is so... new for you."

"I really want to step up to the plate," Tristan told him quietly. "And I think you know that."

Jake's heart hammered in his chest. "I don't know if I can let you."

"I kind of sensed that. That's why I hadn't already asked you out," Tristan admitted with a quiet chuckle. "That, and... I think you deserve someone who's out. You're not just out. You're about to be *really* out, to people who barely know you. I can't support you or help you if I'm... hiding who I am."

Jake caught his breath and took a moment to eat a few fries, trying to turn that one over in his head. "That's a big commitment to make."

"It isn't solely for you," Tristan told him, his expression earnest. Despite his trade, Jake had always sensed that he wasn't putting any pretenses on when speaking to him, and he appreciated that more than anything. "I need to live this life for myself. So whatever happens with my career, it's not your fault. But I've been holding myself back, thinking... well..."

He looked uncomfortable for a moment, so Jake nudged his knee. "Thinking?"

Tristan gulped and laughed. "This doesn't reflect well on me."

"Not everything we do does," Jake said with a little shrug. "I've done, said, thought stupid shit before. You just have to try to get better."

Tristan nodded. He took his own turn eating a few fries, and Jake gave him space to think about what he wanted to say. When he finally spoke, he looked back at Jake and squared his shoulders. "I've been turning down roles because I thought they were too gay. Or because they were outright— the characters, I mean."

"Ah. Right," Jake murmured.

His first instinct was to say, *Too gay? Like that's a bad thing?*

But, God, Tristan was clearly unhappy being closeted. He hadn't said or done anything homophobic to Jake, even as they established their… whatever this was. So Jake was careful, even within his own mind, to avoid passing judgment.

Who the hell was he to decide what was and wasn't right for someone else to do? Getting through life with as little injury as possible was everyone's right.

"Okay," Jake said at last. "I don't like the idea of you being afraid of being gay, but… I don't get the impression you are. So as long as you aren't being an asshole in your real life…"

"But that's just it," Tristan pressed, leaning forward and bracing his elbows on his knees. It was the pose he seemed to adopt when he wanted to really communicate something important to him. "I just needed something to fight for. And I think I've found that."

Jake couldn't meet his gaze. The pleasure inside him was at war with the embarrassment, and the worry. *What if I'm not what he thinks? Or, worse, what if he's trying to be with me out of just… duty?* He tried to hide his blush by frowning down at the bag. "Damn, where did my fries go?"

"Thank you for being so understanding." Tristan sounded relieved now, and much more like himself. He held out his bag. "Want some of mine?"

Jake smiled and shook his head. "Thanks, but I shouldn't. I'm trying to eat healthy, aside from… you know, cravings. For the baby's sake."

Which brought them right back to the elephant in the womb.

"So, um. Do you want to be involved with me, or the baby, or both…?" It shouldn't have been such a terrifying question. Jake's voice shook anyway when he asked.

Tristan didn't even bat an eye before he answered. "Both." The strength and certainty in his answer were undeniable.

"Oh. You and me… I mean, setting aside the baby, if we can," Jake said, laughing. "I think we should talk about what that means."

Tristan scrunched up his now-empty bag and threw it in the can next to the bench. Then, he scooted closer and wrapped his arm around Jake's shoulder. "Can we drive to the beach and talk? Santa Monica?"

Jake caught his breath. "But that's…"

"An hour, if there's traffic? That's fine."

"Out of the blue? That's a lot of effort," Jake teased. "I mean, I'm off work, so it's fine with me…"

Tristan squeezed him around the shoulders. "A lot of effort, but you're worth it."

Again, Jake's cheeks flushed with heat. Somehow, he'd always fantasized about a man—he'd never known who, exactly—saying these things to him.

But he'd never known exactly what it would be like. A small part of him had never expected to *actually* hear them. Now that he did, he didn't know what to do with it.

"Thank you," Jake murmured. "You make me happy. I don't know what we're doing, but I want to talk about it."

He'd never had a guy suggest this kind of spontaneous date, either. He'd spent these last few years so rigidly cooped up that he hadn't let himself be spontaneous. What better time than now?

"Great." Tristan beamed and pulled Jake to his feet. "Your car or mine?"

"I'll drive," Jake told him. "Saves us swapping cars. Let's go."

"Let's go."

As they walked to the car, holding hands yet again, Jake couldn't wipe the smile off his face. This felt like a taster of what he could get.

All he had to do was let himself say yes… and let himself trust. Could he do that much? Jake honestly didn't know the answer, but he hadn't been asked the question yet.

Don't count your chickens before they're hatched.

But, judging by the way Tristan flirted with him and teased him to keep him distracted from the traffic heading out of the city, this chick was already pecking its shell.

The only thing that had been standing in the way—and had been for weeks now—was Jake himself.

CHAPTER
Sixteen

TRISTAN

Just the sound of waves crashing on the beach made the impromptu trip worth it, a hundred times over.

Sitting on the nearly-deserted beach next to Jake, their arms wrapped around one another to stay warm in the brisk spring breeze, was the cherry on top of it all.

They hadn't talked about their relationship for the whole forty-minute drive here, choosing by unspoken agreement to save that for a more romantic moment.

And that was now.

Tristan tried to pretend to himself that his shivers were purely from the ocean breeze. The idea that Jake might just cut the strings and walk off now was utterly terrifying.

And there was a small part of him that worried that all he was good for was being a sperm donor.

He trusted Jake when he'd said it hadn't been deliberate, there was no question about that. But events were set in motion now that they couldn't slow down.

They were both gazing out over the ocean as they

squished their toes in the sand, listening to people on the boardwalk nearby. Finally, Tristan spoke up. It had to be him that started this conversation, because it had been him holding them back from it.

"So… us."

Jake turned an expectant smile to him. "Yeah?"

"I like you," Tristan murmured, keeping his voice down. He didn't quite know why. It wasn't like anyone was right next to them to overhear, and if they were, he wouldn't give a fuck.

Something in him had shifted since meeting Jake. Hell, all of his priorities had changed, and that had happened before Jake even told him about the baby.

Coming out—*living* out—had suddenly become an option, when it never had been before.

"I like you, too," Jake said, chuckling. The way the corners of his eyes crinkled always made Tristan smile. He was developing faint laugh lines, and as far as Tristan was concerned, they were the best beauty mark there was.

"I… I mean, I want to date you." Tristan couldn't hide his nervousness, and he didn't even try. "I haven't dated in a long time. I barely remember how this works. I didn't want to rush things. But we've been getting along so well, and I can't stop thinking about you when we're not together. And I loved sleeping with you. Not just the sex—I mean, actually sleeping." Fuck. He was rambling. Amateur mistake.

But Jake wasn't sparing him and interjecting. He just grinned, letting Tristan keep talking. What a jerk.

"I—I know we were just fuck-buddies, and there weren't supposed to be strings, but… look at us now. I want to romance you. I don't exactly know how, but I want to try." Tristan licked his lips nervously. "If you want to keep it to just, you know, screwing around... I know that's all we were supposed to do..."

Jake pressed a finger to Tristan's lips. "No," he said softly, finally cutting off his ramble. "I did just want to fuck—at first. And then I realized I like you, and I like spending time around you. There's only one problem."

Damn it. Tristan caught his breath. "What?" he urged as fear squeezed in a fist around his heart.

"I'd always imagined myself raising a kid alone." Jake leaned into his shoulder, resting a hand on Tristan's thigh.

Before Tristan panicked, he calmed himself down. They were talking, that was all. He wanted—needed—to understand Jake's point of view. "Why?"

"I didn't think I'd find someone who was interested in sticking around for more than one night. Not because of the trans thing," Jake added, his lips quirking into a smile. "Well... sometimes because of that. But I'm usually pretty confident about it. It's a good asshole filter. I mean, because... a baby. A family. It's a big commitment. I want to know the guy I raise kids with."

"It is," Tristan murmured. God only knew he'd spent enough sleepless hours over the past few nights just thinking about it, trying to see himself as a father. "And that makes sense."

"It does?" Jake relaxed and rested his head on Tristan's shoulder as he let a sigh escape.

"Yeah," Tristan reassured him. "I hear you. And I can't guarantee that we'll stay together forever, you know? Not until we date and we see how we get along. This isn't like a few decades ago when people would get knocked up and get married out of commitment."

"Thank God," Jake laughed. "That's what my parents did,

and look how that turned out." It was the first time he'd directly talked about his parents, but even though Tristan stayed quiet, he didn't clarify.

Tristan squeezed him around the shoulders. "But we have nine months to figure this out, right? Like a trial run. And as long as we're on the same page about the baby, and who's raising them, we can stay friends."

"Absolutely. I don't like just ditching exes because they're exes," Jake said. "Life's too short for that, unless they're assholes."

Tristan chuckled. "Yeah. And I know you'd keep custody, whatever happens. I'm fine doing whatever paperwork we need to do. But I want some kind of involvement."

"Right," Jake agreed. "That's fine. But what if we do stay together, and… I don't know, we disagree on things? That's my biggest fear."

Tristan squeezed him again, encouraging him to talk it out. "Like what?"

"I don't know. Religion? Spanking?"

"I'd agree to spank you until you took the Lord's name in vain." Tristan winked at Jake when Jake gasped and looked at him.

Jake dissolved into giggles in his arms, and it was such a beautiful sound. He sprawled on the sand, laughing until tears came to his eyes.

"See? It would be a crime *not* to date someone as funny as me." Tristan smirked and poked Jake in the chest when he finally sat up again.

"Okay."

Tristan's heart jumped. "O-Okay? As in—"

"Yes, you worrywart." Jake was teasing him now, his eyes

glinting with mischief. "We'll date, and we'll see how it goes while I'm pregnant. After the birth, we'll figure things out. I want you to have a role in this kid's life if you want one, even if things don't work out between us. But I want things to work out. On one condition."

"Of course."

"You buy me a lot of French fries over the next nine months."

Tristan grabbed Jake's cheeks and pulled him in to kiss him as hard as he could. Their lips slid together, firm and sparking with heat. From head to toe, he felt *good* in a way he hadn't before.

Renewed.

"Thank you," he whispered when they finally pulled apart.

Jake swayed for a moment and shook his head, putting a hand on Tristan's shoulder. "No. Thank you for finally asking. I thought you'd never do it."

Tristan drew a breath and let it out. He was still pretty sure he'd gotten the better end of this deal, but he wasn't going to argue. "So did I. Next up... boardwalk?"

"Only if you go on the Ferris wheel with me," Jake told him.

The blood drained from Tristan's face, but he tried to keep a brave expression as he stood up. He was pretty sure he had to fulfill all of his new boyfriend's requests. Hell, that was probably in the *new boyfriend* handbook. "Of course."

"Oh, my God." Of course Jake had noticed. Damn his observant nature. He could be an actor himself. "Tristan Bailey. Are you afraid of heights?"

"Dunno what you mean," Tristan grumbled. "Heights are fine. I'm fine. Around heights."

"You are!" Jake scrambled to his feet and cackled. "You aaaare," he drawled, not letting Tristan get away with it.

Tristan covered his face for a moment, trying to erase the blush he knew stained his cheeks. He rarely blushed—a good trait in an actor who worked with cameras—but Jake's teasing got under his skin. "Fine! I admit it. I am."

"But the world looks amazing from above," Jake gasped. "You're missing out!"

"Why do you like it?" Tristan offered Jake his hand. The newness of that simple act hadn't worn off—and neither had his pride at having this wonderful, sweet, smart man on his arm.

And, eventually, this man who would be the father of his child.

It was more than Tristan had ever hoped for. More than he'd known he *could* hope for. His hopes of having a child, or a family, or even a partner, had been buried for so long that he could hardly believe he was lucky enough to get a chance at it all.

God, he wanted—needed—this to work out. It was the missing puzzle piece that made Tristan's resolve firm: to be himself on- and off-screen, and to be the man Jake needed him to be.

As Tristan listened to Jake explain how he liked feeling like his troubles were down below with the rest of the world, and all its people racing around in little cars, he smiled and let Jake talk.

His bubbly personality was back now, and stronger than ever before. Without the stress of this talk hanging over his head, Tristan felt more like himself, too. He wouldn't have to worry about saying one thing wrong and never hearing back from Jake again.

He could stop thinking about the *what ifs* and *maybes*.

Holy crap. Tristan had a real live boyfriend. Zeph was never, ever gonna believe him when he called him tonight.

CHAPTER
Seventeen

JAKE, THREE WEEKS LATER

Our one-month anniversary is next week! Chinese and a walk in the park?

Jake had to reread that text a few times before it sank in. He laughed and covered his face as he left his phone in the break room, ready for another busy shift at the restaurant.

The franchise manager, Ned, was in today. Jake always tried to do his best when the manager was around, even more than usual. He took great pride in doing whatever he did well, and that included work, even when he'd rather be daydreaming about his new boyfriend.

It was early days, but one month was a promising sign. Jake was pretty proud that he hadn't run away screaming yet, and he hadn't scared Tristan off, either. The idea of a couple celebrating a month together had always made Jake laugh, but now... he understood. Every month that passed brought changes to Jake's life, and to Tristan's, too.

Celebrating every month that passed was utterly adorable, and just like Tristan.

Where Jake was practical, and had made a list and

checked it twice to deal with the upcoming nine months, his boyfriend felt his way through the world. It wasn't a bad combination. In fact, as far as a coparenting arrangement went, it seemed like it would work very well.

Over the last three weeks, they'd had the best of both worlds: hot sex and emotional intimacy. With a healthy dose of public affection, too. At last, Jake was kind of sold on this relationship thing.

"Who's that making you giggle?" Amanda teased as she followed him out of the staff room.

"You should know."

Amanda smirked. "Oooh. That's right. The hot boyfriend. Why isn't he around anymore?"

"He's got work. Steady, actually. It's a big movie part," Jake told her, grinning.

Amanda lit up and clapped his arm. "Oh, that's wonderful, sweetie! Congratulations!"

Jake grimaced at the pet name. Certain names were okay by him. Others, like *honey* and *sweetie*… they just reminded him of a time in his life he'd much rather forget. Hearing them said by someone other than his parents, and not sarcastically, still made those moments echo far too loudly in his head. It felt like a stupid hang-up to have, but everyone had their baggage.

"Thank you," he answered absently as he punched his user ID into the POS system. "It kind of sucks. He'll be working long hours for the most of the trimester."

It took him a few moments before he realized what he'd said, and he sucked in his breath, looking over at Amanda. That wasn't a unit of measurement most people used.

She'd heard it, too. Her jaw dropped as she looked down at his stomach and back up, her face containing the question.

Jake chuckled sheepishly. "I wasn't gonna tell people, but… yes."

"Oh, my God!" Amanda tried to muffle her squeal as she hugged him. "That's amazing. I had no idea you could even—that you wanted—congratulations! Oh, wow."

They both nearly jumped apart when they heard Ned's voice, all brisk and business. "Amanda. Table five is looking for you."

"Sorry." Amanda rolled her eyes at Jake, but Jake waved her off. Service came first, after all.

It felt kind of nice not to have that secret. He was goddamn tired of secrets, and now that there were fewer than ever before in his life, he'd grown used to not having to think twice about what he said, and to whom.

On the other hand, the look Ned gave him as he passed was inscrutable.

Had he overheard? What did he think?

Jake couldn't afford to stop and worry about it, though. He had work to get to. The place was packed to the seams already. If his chest was weirdly sore and the smell of food was mildly repulsive, that was just too bad.

If it got worse, he had no idea how he'd deal with it, but he'd find a way. He smelled food all day. His job required it. And he needed the job.

He wasn't the first pregnant person to rely on work at a restaurant, diner, or coffee shop. There had to be tips and tricks on working through morning sickness.

Who needed a mom for advice when he had the internet on his side? Jake added that to his mental list of things to Google when he got home.

So far, it had done wonders, as long as he was willing to overlook the fact that every resource casually assumed that anyone who was pregnant was a woman, had breasts, and had a steady male partner. It was alienating to have to run everything through a mental filter of whether or not it applied to him.

Another group of guests walked through the door, and Jake headed over to them with a cheerful smile. Time to get his ass in gear.

***

"Jake? Can I have a word?"

Before Jake could even pick up his phone from the break room, Ned was calling him into the office. "Sure, give me three seconds." Once he'd changed shoes and loaded up his pockets with wallet, car keys, and phone, he followed Ned into the office.

His stomach dropped as soon as Ned closed the door and sat down, his expression solemn. He'd been let go from enough jobs to know how this went.

"I'm afraid I'm going to have to let you go, Jake. We won't be needing you to come in tomorrow. I'll have HR get in touch to wrap up the loose ends."

Well, Ned wasn't beating around the bush. Jake opened and shut his mouth wordlessly for a few moments, trying to make heads or tails of this. "I... Why?"

"Because I need to let you go."

You need to let me go because you need to let me go? Jake's bullshit detector was giving him a huge red flag at that answer. When they avoided the question, it was because it was legally problematic. "What do you mean? Is it my performance?"

"I can't answer those questions," Ned answered coolly. "As

you're probably aware, California is an at-will state…"

"I know what that means," Jake interrupted. If he was getting fired, he didn't care about being rude. "But is it something I could have done better?"

He resisted the tears that threatened to build up in his eyes. *Fuck. The last thing I need is pregnancy hormones hitting right now, thanks very much,* he thought.

"I'm happy to give you a positive reference for a future employer," Ned answered.

Okay, he wasn't getting anywhere with this. Jake smiled tightly and nodded once, refusing to let himself get emotional in front of Ned. "Thanks. Bye."

Amanda tried to talk to him, but he power-walked out of the restaurant, too afraid of his reaction if he stuck around.

She chased him to the parking lot. "Shit. Jake, are you okay?"

Jake's eyes were blurry now as he wiped them with his arm, leaning on his car. "Yes. No. Sort of. I just got fired."

"What?" Amanda exclaimed. "That's… that's bullshit. Why?"

"He wouldn't tell me. They knew I was trans and they didn't have a problem until now. But…" Jake trailed off, ducking his head.

He'd been stupid to think it was safe to talk about it at work. One careless slip of the tongue, and he was out of a job.

And, critically, the healthcare that job had offered.

"It's the pregnancy," Amanda surmised in a whisper. "Shit. That's illegal!"

Jake laughed bitterly. He'd lost more than one job while transitioning, even though that was illegal. People lost their jobs all the time for technically illegal reasons. Proving it was a whole different story. "Good luck to me, getting any enforcement on that."

"That's awful," Amanda shook her head, folding her arms. "If there's anything I can do…"

Jake nodded jerkily. "For a job I might not have been able to do in a couple months' time… I guess it's not the worst thing." *Don't think of the healthcare. Don't think of rent. It'll work out, somehow.* He gulped hard. "I better get going."

She pulled him in for a tight hug and made him promise to text her and let her know how things went, and then he was on the road.

An unemployed, pregnant man. People didn't like hiring pregnant women—who the hell would hire a pregnant man? But he didn't have the money or the energy to fight it in court, or whatever the next step was. He'd never bothered with that.

Better to move on.

God, life seemed to be several steps ahead of him the whole way. He'd been wanting to get pregnant, but not yet? Boom, early pregnancy. He'd wanted to get a better job? He lost this one. This year was turning into a terrifyingly high-speed treadmill he'd just been dumped on.

At least he had a boyfriend for moral support, but he couldn't cry on Tristan's shoulder until he was done work— and he was putting in long days of filming.

Jake felt utterly alone, his back against the wall. Sure, he did well in that spot, but why the hell should he have to?

Fuck everything about this. The worst part was that he couldn't even drown his sorrows in a glass of wine.

An Oreo McFlurry it was. And if anyone looked weirdly at him for eating a McFlurry in a parking lot and crying, they could go fuck themselves.

CHAPTER
Eighteen
TRISTAN

For a first read-through, Tristan was pretty damn happy with how his day had gone. Sure, they'd been stop-and-start at the beginning as they talked through the nature of the script and the director's ideas, but it felt like they were all on the same page. Literally and creatively.

They'd already arranged to meet up for drinks on Friday, too. Tristan was very aware that, as one of the leads, it was his responsibility to encourage a friendly and warm atmosphere on set. His costar, Brian, seemed to agree, judging by his enthusiastic agreement when Tristan had suggested drinks.

"Aw, shit," he whispered when he saw a string of texts from Jake. Even though he kept his phone in the car unless it would overheat, Jake tried not to send him too many texts while he was at work. If he ever saw more than one or two, it was a bad thing.

He only needed to skim them before he knew where he was headed: Jake's house.

Jake got *fired*? What the hell had happened?

The whole drive there, he hoped Jake wasn't in bed, but he had the feeling that even if he were, he'd welcome company.

"Hey, babe," he greeted as soon as Jake opened the door. Jake fell into his arms, and Tristan squeezed him as tightly as he could. "Oh, Jake. Fuck. I'm sorry."

Jake sniffled, but he seemed determined to keep himself composed. "Come on in. Thank you for coming over. It's earlier than I expected."

"We just did the first read-through today," Tristan told him quietly. "Stefan—that's the director—wanted to talk to production people about stuff before he asked us for ideas."

His mind was already in gear. Could he get Jake a job on set? He'd ask tomorrow if there were any unfilled positions. Sometimes people had to drop out and production needed a replacement…

"Oh. Did it go okay?" Jake shut the door and led Tristan to his couch. Judging by the tissue box, bags of chips, and huge bottle of Coke, he'd been on the couch for a while.

"Yeah," Tristan said. He tried to keep it casual, not wanting to rub in the fact that he was working and Jake wasn't. If he could just get Jake a few qualifying jobs, he could get the benefits of the union, and healthcare, and…

Oh, fuck. Healthcare.

He sat down and pulled Jake into him. "Are you okay?"

Jake sounded miserable. "I don't know. Am I? I will be. I've been fired before, for stupid shit. I always get jobs again. People don't care if you're a serial job-switcher as long as they can exploit you in their shitty restaurant for a few shitty months."

"Oh, hon—" Tristan murmured, then winced. "Sorry."

Jake just sighed. The fact that he didn't even get annoyed

was a bad sign. Tristan still didn't know why some words were allowed and others weren't, but Jake usually got twitchy after he used the wrong one.. Clearly he was a lot more distressed than he was trying to let on.

"Do you know why?" Tristan pressed. "Are you sure it was legal?"

Jake gave a bitter laugh. "I'm sure it *wasn't* legal. Obviously."

"Yeah," Tristan chuckled sheepishly. "Sorry. I didn't mean to imply you were screwing up at work or anything. But if it's not legal, that means…"

"What, I can go to court?" Jake challenged.

Tristan tilted his head at the defiance in Jake's tone. "Well, yeah."

"As if. The time and money and getting a lawyer and figuring out how to complain, and I might not even be able to prove anything." Jake rested his head on Tristan's shoulder again quietly, and a band of emotions tightened around Tristan's heart.

God, I wanna yell at those assholes. "How did it…? Just randomly?"

"I accidentally let on to Amanda I'm pregnant. The manager, Ned, overheard. He pulled me in at the end of the shift." Even Jake's words were soft, like he'd given up on caring.

As hard as it was to talk to him when he was all sharp edges, it was so much harder to see him uncharacteristically quiet.

Defeated.

"So it's definitely discrimination," Tristan concluded, biting his tongue for a few moments to stop himself from cursing them out. That might make him feel better, but it wouldn't help Jake. "I'm sorry, baby. They didn't deserve you."

"Clearly, they agreed." Jake rubbed his cheek against Tristan's shoulder, and Tristan caressed his hair.

"You know what I meant," Tristan murmured quietly. "You're too fucking good for them."

"Yeah. I just feel dumb for having let it slip. I could have gone another month or two before I started to show—and even then, I could have written it off as a pot belly. Nobody suspects a dude of being pregnant, even a trans dude."

Tristan nodded. "Are you gonna look for something else?"

"I don't have a lot of choice. But I don't know how long it will take, and…" Jake trailed off.

Tristan pulled Jake gently down until his head rested on his lap and rubbed his shoulder and arm. "I'll help find something if I can."

"No. I can manage."

Tristan smiled fondly down at Jake, whose eyes were closed as Tristan stroked his hair. That damn stubborn streak of his. It was one of the things he most loved about him, yet the very same part of him that made it hard to get close.

Tristan had to have patience and hope that Jake would come around.

"I'd still like to help."

"We'll see when we get there," Jake murmured, not giving him an inch. He never did in disagreements, and it made Tristan smile. At least he wasn't that quiet, defeated man Tristan had glimpsed a minute ago. This was more like himself.

"It might not be a problem. You oughta get the next job

you walk in about," Tristan agreed with a smile. "With your charming smile…"

The teasing stirred Jake to life, at least. He opened his eyes as he laughed up at Tristan. "I see you trying to flirt."

"I'm not *trying* to flirt," Tristan told him, clicking his tongue smugly. "I'm succeeding. Look at that blush."

Jake hadn't actually been blushing, but now he was. God, he was easy to tease.

"Shut up," Jake laughed, covering his face.

Just seeing him a little happier, if only for a few moments, made Tristan smile back at him. "Never. And you wouldn't like me to, really."

"No," Jake agreed, sitting up again and pecking his lips. "You're right about that. When's call time?"

"Eight. More production meetings."

"Not too early, then. We can lie in for an hour or two if we go to bed now," Jake suggested.

"I think I know what you're thinking," Tristan winked.

He'd been surprised at how high Jake's libido was. For some reason, he'd assumed pregnancy and sex were incompatible. Apparently, it was exactly the opposite. Some days, Jake seemed lukewarm to the idea. But more days than not, he was practically peeling Tristan's clothes off before they closed the door.

"Do you?" Jake raised a brow. "That it's time to size up?"

Well, now he was hard. Tristan squirmed as Jake's hand ran up his thigh. "To the other dick you showed me?" He was getting used to Jake's usual cock now. The bigger one had just been sitting there for some time on the shelf, like a promise.

"If you're very, very good," Jake teased. He stood up and

offered Tristan a hand. When Tristan took it, he found himself being pulled to the bedroom.

If this was the best way he could offer Jake a distraction, then he'd just have to do it. Completely selflessly, of course. It was a hard job, but someone had to take it on.

Tristan nearly tripped over his feet in his eagerness to get to the bedroom. "I didn't expect this," he admitted. "I figured there'd be more ice cream and less…"

"Creaming?"

"Yes," Tristan laughed. "I like the way you cope, though."

Jake grinned as he shut the door. "Strip and kneel."

His tone was casual, yet firm. This was the Jake that Tristan knew and loved so much—not that he didn't love him when he was down, but he worried so much about him, too.

This Jake was the guy who would flip off the haters and make something even bigger and better of himself in the end. Tristan could hardly wait to see what he did.

"Yes, sir." Tristan took a minute to peel his clothes off, letting Jake slowly get an eyeful at a time as he pulled off his shirt, pants, and underwear. By the time he'd yanked the last sock off, he was half-hard, and it was obvious.

When he sank to his knees, he looked up at Jake for approval.

"I love that you love being bossed around." Jake sighed a noise of satisfaction and nodded at him, licking his lips. The slide of that pert pink tongue across his delicate lips made Tristan all the hungrier to taste them.

Tristan, for his part, was more confident now than he'd ever been. The less he had to hide and the more secure he felt in what he had and who he was, the easier it was to be assertive. Hell, he'd held his ground during the read-through once today and gotten the director to side with him on the dynamics of one scene.

But being able to give all that up for a few hours and let Jake call the shots was incredibly satisfying in a way he couldn't describe if he'd tried. So he hadn't—not even to Zeph.

It wasn't exactly kinky, but there was a clear dominance and submission in all of their sexual interactions that made him feel like he was the bottom, no matter whose equipment was doing what.

God, Tristan relished it.

Jake dropped his pants and underwear, and he opened the drawer that Tristan knew held his harness. It took all he had not to squirm with anticipation as Jake swapped out his everyday dick for his harness, picked up the larger cock, and slid it through the ring.

It took a couple of minutes before the harness was fastened and leather straps dangled alongside his thighs, the black strips framing his hipbones like ribbons against his pale skin. Every passing second only dialed up the anticipation for Tristan.

He was totally hard now, without even having touched himself. God, sex with Jake was like nothing he'd experienced before. It had only gotten better as they grew familiar with each other's bodies and tastes.

"Now," Jake said as he turned back to him, letting him see the result. The length jutting up along Jake's stomach made Tristan moan quietly with desire. Jake tugged his shirt off, finally joining Tristan in getting naked. "Where were we?"

"Fucking me?" Tristan asked, perking up. He knelt up a little straighter for good measure.

Jake smiled, his expression fond as he cupped himself in

one hand to support the length and weight of his cock, and walked closer. "I don't know if I can get off with this one. It's pretty new."

"Oooh. Like, brand-new?"

"I've only used it on me," Jake said, smiling as he grabbed a condom.

They'd been exclusive for a few months now, and they'd gotten tested, especially given the health considerations that Jake needed to make. They'd decided already that they wouldn't use condoms for Tristan's cock.

Packers were an exception, though. Something about the effect of lube on them. Tristan hadn't really been paying attention when he'd asked, too distracted—as he was now—by the sight of it, and what that did to him.

"Does a new cock make you a virgin all over again?" Tristan grinned up at Jake.

Jake hummed. "I don't know. You'll have to see if I fuck you like a virgin."

God, hearing him talk dirty turned Tristan on. He gasped as Jake cupped his cheek and guided the tip of his cock to his mouth. Jake thrust gently a few times, his gaze intent on the length disappearing between his lips.

Since Jake couldn't feel this, it was all about how it looked. So Tristan tilted his head just right to give Jake a great show. After bobbing his head a few times, he opened his mouth wide and let the tip press against the inside of his cheek, gazing up at Jake.

"Bed," Jake ordered, his voice a low growl. *Oh, hell, yes,* Tristan thought. When Jake talked like this, it meant he was going to fuck him hard.

Tristan's body burned with anticipation, already clenching with anticipation. He ached to have something inside him. He scrambled to his feet and bent over the edge of the bed, spreading his legs.

But Jake turned him over, guiding him further up the bed so he could lie on his back. "I want to see you," Jake murmured.

In a rare moment of modesty, Tristan blushed. He glanced down, but the shyness didn't last long when Jake pushed his knees up to his chest and grabbed the lube.

"Oh, fuck, yes." He'd long since learned that Jake was good with his fingers. *Really* good.

Jake grinned as he slid two wet fingers inside, going gently at first and then a little harder. By the time he crooked them to rub against the prostate, sparks of pleasure were shooting across Tristan's skin, and it was all he could do not to follow them with his load.

Holding out long enough was a real challenge when Jake seemed determined to push him to the limits and then some, but Tristan relished it.

"Fuck me," he finally begged when those fingers didn't feel like enough. He needed more inside him.

Jake's cock pressed against him moments later, and then inside him, and Tristan was floating in the ecstasy of being so full it hurt, yet wanting more.

And, inch by inch, he got it.

"It's so good," Tristan panted against Jake's lips when Jake ducked his head between Tristan's knees to kiss him.

"I knew you were a size queen," Jake gently teased.

Tristan nodded hard. "All the way." Jake had been right that night a few months ago, when he'd said that being with him came with benefits that most guys couldn't bring to the table. The U-Pick cocks were one of them.

Jake gave a few slow thrusts, keeping it lazy at first, but

that didn't last long. Before Tristan could beg for it, Jake seemed to read his body and the way he tried to push up and into him.

Within minutes, the bed squeaked under them, but all Tristan could hear was his own whimpers and moans as Jake pounded him into the bed. He was so deep inside, and filled Tristan so damn perfectly, that Jake couldn't imagine sex with anyone else again.

How the hell had he ever thought this could get boring?

"Yes," Tristan gasped, the telltale jolts of pleasure running through him. "Fuck, baby. I'm so close. You're gonna make me come."

Jake tangled his fingers in Tristan's hair and leaned in to lick his throat. It was a raw, dominant move that hit Tristan's pleasure center exactly where he needed it. "Come for me," Jake whispered.

Tristan was already there. He gasped and arched as his climax hit him before he could even answer, sweeping away every other thought besides the cock that was plunging deep into him, and the lips against his throat, and the hand that rested gently on his hip to keep him steady as he squirmed.

Fuck. That was amazing.

Tristan swallowed a few times as he started to come back to Earth, giving Jake a dizzy grin. "Your turn."

Jake had already pulled out, and in a few deft moves, he wriggled out of the harness. "Working on it," he assured Tristan with a grin.

"Let me suck you off," Tristan whispered. He shifted until he lay flat on the bed, and then grabbed Jake's hips to guide him up his body until Tristan straddled his head.

He closed his lips around Jake's cock and sucked it into his mouth, flicking his tongue quickly back and forth over the head as Tristan thrust into his mouth, ground his hips, and groaned.

It turned him on so much to see Jake throwing himself into this that he was already starting to plan round two in the morning.

When Jake came, gasping for breath and whispering his name over and over like a mantra, Tristan rubbed his hip and gradually let go of the suction, slowing down his tongue until he licked the sensitive nub a few last times and flopped back against the pillow.

"I love you," Jake whispered. Then, he blushed bright red and scrambled up. "Better wash up and get to bed."

Tristan caught him by the hand before he could run and grinned at him. "I love you, too, sexy. I'll love you even more if you bring me back a washcloth to clean up."

And when Jake did, and they'd cleaned up and climbed under the covers and turned the lights off, Tristan kissed him until Jake's eyes closed with exhaustion and satisfaction. Jake's breathing fell into an easy, deep rhythm, and Tristan stroked his hair until his own eyelids grew heavy.

Love is the easiest thing in the world. It felt like the hardest to find sometimes, but now that I have, it's as easy as breathing.

He fell asleep to the sound of those deep, easy breaths.

Whatever he'd done to deserve a man like Jake in his bed and his heart and his life, he didn't know... but he was grateful nonetheless. And he always would be, whatever hard times they hit along the way.

Jake had been expecting the call all day. Not the call from a new employer wanting to offer him a job based on his impressive resume or great interview… no, the call from the insurance company.

Sure enough, there it was. It was the first day of a new month, which meant his insurance had ended. His eight-week pregnancy checkup had been that morning. If the doctor's office tried to file the claim, he'd figured insurance would bounce it back to him.

"Thanks for the heads-up. I'll pay by credit card, please."

After he hung up with the doctor's office, Tristan glanced over at him from the kitchen. He'd been spending more and more time at Tristan's place instead of his own, to the point where Tristan had told him he was getting another key cut.

That, at least, was one small bright spot.

"Who was that?"

"The doctor."

"Shit. Your insurance, right?" Tristan wiped his hands on the tea towel and joined Jake on the couch.

He'd just put something delicious-smelling in the oven. Jake just hoped his appetite kept up. Sometimes the moment he started to eat, his stomach decided that it didn't like food after all.

The internet told him the nausea would be worst for the first trimester, and he just hoped it was right. In the mornings, before he left for work, Tristan would bring him weak tea and plain crackers, and that was often all he could manage—if that—until noon.

That limited his job options, and even his job-hunting options, but he still had rent to pay.

Unless Tristan offered him a place to live, which he seemed to be pushing for. Jake hadn't let the conversation come up yet, so he didn't have to shoot Tristan down, but he wouldn't be surprised to get an offer.

"If you can't get another job… and even if you do, it might not have insurance benefits…" Tristan trailed off. He twisted his hands together, and then took Jake's. "Okay, I know you won't like this, but… we might need to get you on my insurance plan. Which is a big question to pop right now."

It took Jake a second to understand what he meant, and then to decide how he felt about it.

Part of him said *yes,* and part of him said *what the hell,* and part of him said… well, no, actually. No part of him said *no.* Just that marrying a guy he'd been dating for two months was a dumb idea.

But was it, really? They'd only had minor hiccups for these last couple of months. So far, they'd resolved them all over a cup of coffee, or sometimes in bed.

"It makes sense," Jake said slowly. "For everyone's sake."

Tristan lit up and started smiling ear-to-ear. "Yeah. It does." Then, in that way that meant he was trying not to be overeager, he schooled his expression and cleared his throat. "I mean, it's just logical."

He's hoping it means more, too. Jake grinned at him and took his hand. "Look, I wouldn't normally do this kind of thing, but... I'm willing to consider it. I can't afford to have a baby uninsured, and I can't afford individual insurance right now. Especially if they'll consider my pregnancy a preexisting condition. You just need to call your plan and ask—"

"Already done," Tristan admitted, ducking his head sheepishly. "Sorry. But I didn't want to give you a false sense of hope."

Jake melted a little. Tristan loved him enough to plan for his comfort, even in this utterly ridiculous situation. "If it breaks down relationship-wise... I know we've been dating two months, but we have to plan this if we're going to jump straight in," Jake finally said.

"I was thinking this through. If we stop dating, we'll stay legally married until you have pediatric care settled one way or another." Tristan looked serious now.

"You'd do that? I mean, you wouldn't exactly be able to date anyone else while you're in marriage limbo."

Tristan smiled at him and shook his head. "Yeah, but I don't want to."

"Even if this ended?"

Tristan put his arm around Jake's shoulder and drew him in to kiss his forehead. "It'll take me a lifetime to forget you, Jake Gray."

Jake let out a breath he didn't know he'd been holding. He put his head down on Tristan's shoulder, trying to hide his smile. "Okay. But if we do this... we probably have to live together."

"That's the thing I was worried you'd turn down."

Jake smiled as he looked up at him. "You were going to propose marriage to me, and you were worried I wouldn't move in with you?"

Then, he laughed before Tristan could even answer. Come to think of it, Tristan knew him way too well. Moving in meant reliance on Tristan, but marriage didn't necessarily. It could be strictly a legal arrangement.

Tristan grinned. "Was I wrong?"

Jake couldn't stop laughing. "No," he admitted. "I see where you're coming from. God, my life is weird."

"Mine's a little out of the ordinary, too," Tristan teased. "But you know I like it that way."

"What about the move? I'm such a mess lately," Jake groaned. "I don't know if I can move furniture, and... oh, man. I'd need to sell most of the furniture. And boxes. I'll just puke on everything."

Tristan squeezed him tightly. "That's what I'm here for. I'll take care of everything I can," he promised. "All you need for now is you, and your clothes, and... your hair stuff, I guess. And your prenatal vitamins."

Jake laughed and kissed Tristan. "So you're offering to marry me, move me into your house, and pamper me? Did I die and go to heaven?"

"I know this is all just... legal stuff, for your sake and the baby's sake," Tristan said. His voice was hesitant in that way that always made Jake pay attention, because it meant he had something big to say. "But I kind of hope it would mean more, too. In time. A lot of people have rushed into something like this, and... forged true love that way."

"From going through something like this together," Jake agreed softly. "Two dumb kids making a life together."

It was a romantic idea, he had to admit. Just because his

parents had done it, and had done such a bad job toward the end, didn't mean that was his own path.

Hell, Tristan didn't seem to talk much with his own parents, but he was devoted and thorough already with the prenatal details in a way that made Jake trust him to be a good influence in the kid's life after birth, too.

And that was the highest commendation he could give anyone. Trusting them to take part in the dream he'd held for his whole life said more to him than any amount of hot sex, or fun bantering, or even Chinese in the park.

"Let's do it."

"I never imagined I'd have a courthouse wedding," Jake whispered into Tristan's ear.

He didn't know why he was whispering. There were just two couples ahead of them in line now, and everyone else was absorbed in talking to each other.

"Me neither. Hell, I didn't think anyone would marry me." Tristan snorted and squeezed his hand. "But here we are. All I had to do was…" He trailed off, showing some discretion.

Knock me up? Jake giggled at the unsaid words.

It was all so much faster than he'd imagined.

At least here in California, they could get a confidential certificate. That way, relatives, agents, fans, tabloids… nobody could snoop on them and find out all the details. A couple hours later, here they were… about to tie the knot.

Jake's heart hammered, and that raised yet another question. If it was all for legal benefits, why did he feel so damn over the moon?

One more couple ahead of them.

"I love you," he whispered, glancing up at Tristan.

Tristan let go of his hand and wrapped his arms around Jake's shoulders. "I love you, too."

I hope he stays with me until the baby's born... and afterward. Forever. Jake hugged Tristan hard—hoping it was hard enough to convey what he felt.

Tristan grunted and squeezed him back with a quiet laugh. "You okay? You sure about this?"

"Yeah. Never better." Jake kissed his cheek and let go again so he could take his hand. "And I've never been more sure of anything. Except maybe running away to L.A., and look where that got me."

Tristan smiled. "You ever think that maybe this is all an elaborate dream?"

"And one day you'll wake up and go back to your normal life?" Jake asked, his heart aching.

"No. One day I'll wake up and you won't be there, and..." Tristan trailed off, clearing his throat and glancing away. "Anyway."

Tears pricked the corners of Jake's eyes. He laced their fingers together and squeezed Tristan's hand. "I'll be here," he promised quietly. "Whether or not we do this. But before we go in, I want to know: is this because you're afraid I'll leave?"

Tristan sucked a slow breath in and gazed at Jake, his brows furrowing. "No. This is the best way I can think of to protect you right now. Are you afraid *I'll* leave?"

"Yes," Jake whispered. "It's not why I said yes to this, but... I'm worried the best thing I've ever known will just fade away."

"Like hell would I ever." Tristan raised Jake's hand and brushed his lips along the back of Jake's hand. "Just watch me."

When their names were called, a smile burst across Jake's face.

It might not be conventional, but when had he ever been?

His heart settled and his mind made up, he walked forward, holding Tristan's hand, to change the course of his life forever for a second time.

But this time, he and Tristan were doing it with eyes wide open, and that meant all the more.

Twenty

TRISTAN

They had exactly one day to move Jake out of his old place and start this new adventure.

That day was dictated by both Jake's rolling lease and Tristan's schedule. Thank God he *had* a day off that worked, but all he could do was hope the weather wouldn't turn unseasonably bad, and hope that everyone showed up.

But just as they'd promised, there was a knock on Jake's front door—soon to be someone else's front door—bright and early.

"I'll get it!" Tristan called out, not wanting Jake to move from the couch. That was the last remaining piece of furniture, and it was getting sold in about an hour.

He'd tried to get Jake to stay at home, but it had already been a battle to get him to accept this much help.

"Surprise!" It was Sam, beaming at him and leading everyone—Kyle, River, Zeph, and Denver. Each of them hugged Tristan as they passed by.

"Hey! Thank you guys," Tristan greeted them. "God, I owe you so much pizza and beer."

"I'll hold you to that!" Sam exclaimed as the others laughed. He had the appetite of an early twenty-something, and he was a lot stronger than he looked.

So were all of them. Between them, Tristan had no doubt they could move these scattered boxes and bags, ditch the stuff to be thrown away, and shift the furniture to be sold into the buyers' trucks and cars.

They got to work without delay, everyone taking care to be quiet when they worked in the living room. Tristan had given them a heads-up about the morning sickness, and it made him glad to see they were being so considerate.

Jake clearly felt bad, because Tristan kept having to get him to lie down again whenever he got up to try to help.

"Honestly, babe, it'll be easy if we get a rhythm going." Tristan didn't want to say, *And if you have to go throw up, that'll throw our rhythm off.*

Jake clearly heard his meaning, though. He pouted as he settled down again, wrapping the blanket around himself. "Yeah. I should have stayed at your place. I'm sorry."

"It's okay." Tristan kissed his forehead. He just wished there were more he could do to help him feel better, besides bring him tea and wait out these next few weeks.

He brought Jake home on their first trip, and got him settled in bed while River and Zeph unpacked the car and necked in public.

"Is he okay?" Zeph finally asked when the two of them noticed Tristan rolling his eyes and sidling past them to grab the last box out of the car.

"He'll be fine, yeah. It tends to hit him worst until noon."

"So, morning sickness," River said. They and Zeph exchanged a glance.

Tristan finally sighed. "Don't tell the world, but yeah, he's pregnant. That's why I wanted him to move in."

Zeph clapped his hands over his mouth. "And you're…"

"Yeah, the baby's mine. But even if it weren't, it's mine now," Tristan told them, tilting his chin up. He defied anyone to tell him he couldn't be a damn good father nevertheless.

Zeph clapped his shoulder. "You're a good man, Tristan. I'm glad you're staying with him."

Tristan nearly laughed. If they only knew the truth—that it was Jake calling the shots here, and him hoping Jake let him stay around.

They didn't even know about the marriage. He and Jake had agreed to keep that under wraps until they were sure that they wanted the world to know. The last thing he needed was the doubts of others nibbling away at the edges of this tentative, beautiful thing they were building.

They'd agreed to keep calling each other boyfriends unless it was to the insurance companies or doctors. Less pressure than suddenly being husbands.

"As long as he wants me to stick around, I will," Tristan told them, and then closed the car door. "Just this last box and we're good for another trip."

Jake didn't own much, luckily. Before late afternoon, they were all done and sharing pizza and beers.

It was weird for Jake to stay in bed past noon, but the place didn't have a lot of privacy. With the sliding master bedroom doors closed, that was about as private as it got. Tristan couldn't exactly go check on him without everyone hearing about it.

He left Jake be until he after saw his friends out, hugging them all and thanking them again.

When he finally slid open the door, he didn't expect Jake to be curled up in bed, silent but unmistakably in tears.

"Oh, hon."

He realized the mistake the moment he'd said it. Goddamn it, why couldn't his brain keep up with his mouth?

"Don't call me that," Jake groaned, pulling his pillow over his face. "Fuck. Just… leave me alone."

Tristan touched his arm under the comforter—or what he hoped was an arm-shaped lump. "Sorry. Do you need anything?"

"To know this isn't a big mistake?" Jake's voice was muffled behind the pillow.

I can't promise it isn't. But that would be the wrong thing to say, Tristan felt. "It's not. We're doing the right thing for both of us, and for our kid."

"Go away and let me cry."

"Okay, babe. I'll get you some more ginger ale and crackers for this week." Tristan kissed the top of Jake's head and headed out, as much as every ounce of him wanted to stay.

He didn't know what was eating Jake up—if it was just hormones, or if something had happened, or if he was upset about moving in.

The possibilities made him think way too much, so he grabbed his car keys and headed for the store instead.

Jake was living with him now. Whatever was wrong, Tristan could do his best to fix it, and he could take care of him in the morning and at night. He wouldn't have to rely on text messages and stealing precious, fleeting minutes with Jake before he had to leave for his own apartment.

For now, Tristan had to have enough faith for—and in— them both.

Tristan announced himself as he walked into the room. "I have ginger ale, and I'm crawling into bed and not leaving until you talk to me."

Oops. Jake had been napping, but he jolted awake at the sound of Tristan's voice.

"Wha'...?" He rubbed his eyes as he pushed the pillow away from his face and looked between Tristan and the glass of ginger ale he'd just put on the bedside table. "For me?"

"Unless you know of another boyfriend with morning sickness I need to be taking care of." Tristan walked around the foot of the bed to climb onto the other side.

Jake sighed and sank back against the pillows, scooting closer to Tristan. He wouldn't look at him, but at least he was smiling. "Nobody crazy enough to do this except me."

"And me," Tristan murmured, resting his hand on Jake's shoulder.

Jake slid closer, and Tristan let him dictate how close he wanted to get. He ended up almost wrapped around Tristan. "I'm sorry I freaked out. Again."

"We can blame the hormones if you want," Tristan said, kissing his temple.

Jake chuckled and shook his head. "Thanks for the offer, but... you should know. All of this has just scared the hell out of me. The last time I was dependent on anyone was my parents."

Here it came. Tristan had been expecting to hear about this someday, but not necessarily now. He prepared himself to add another couple names to his shit list. "Mm?" He petted Jake's hair in the gentle way he'd figured out calmed him down.

The tension drained from Jake's body as Tristan touched him. "Yeah. I was staying with a friend after I graduated high school. They told me not to come home until my *phase* passed, and I realized I'm nothing special. That I'm always going to be a girl."

Tristan winced and tried not to crunch Jake against his side as he squeezed him. "Fuck."

"Yeah. So I called their bluff." Jake said it simply, but it made Tristan smile. "I moved to L.A., started crashing with roommates and working crappy jobs... went on hormones six months later."

"And never looked back?" Tristan chuckled.

Jake shook his head. "Oh, I looked back a lot. I was terrified it was the wrong thing. Sometimes I wasn't even sure about hormones. I'd had to be so certain about myself for so long, in order to try to change their minds—not that that worked. When I was finally allowed to just breathe and think, I started feeling the doubts I wasn't allowed to feel for so long. And getting scared that I was doing something I'd regret later. Part of that was being scared I couldn't have kids, so when I found out I might be able to..."

"And do you? Regret it, I mean?"

"Nah." Jake smiled. He drew a deep breath and let it out. "I can be a man who bears kids, whatever stupid Facebook and the internet have to say about it. All your *if men could have kids, everything would be better* memes. News flash: we can, and it fucking sucks even worse for us, because there's nothing for us. No menswear for pregnant bodies. No daddy blogs to track our weekly progress. No forums to ask for help when I wake up in the middle of the night, terrified my breasts will grow back. Everything is *oh, only ladies get pregnant*. And if you ever say a word, everyone goes, *Oh, but I didn't mean you.* No, of course not. They forget about us. They mean if *real* men could have kids there'd be more respect, not us. As soon as we use our wombs, we're all girls together, right? Pregnant men already exist, and we don't get shit, let alone respect."

In these last few months, Tristan had never heard Jake spill these thoughts. He'd always seemed so strong and certain of himself and unfazed by the assumptions he had to shrug off from healthcare professionals.

"Fuck, Jake," Tristan whispered, gritting his teeth. All he could do was hold Jake and listen, and try not to cry. Wetness leaked through the shoulder of Tristan's t-shirt, right under Jake's cheek. "You never said it was bothering you."

But it made sense. Jake was so used to being strong and unafraid and certain of himself that he might never let on a hint of doubt if Tristan didn't watch for it. Indeed, Tristan had to learn to love Jake the way he needed him to.

Jake was so used to being strong and shutting people out that Tristan had to be stronger sometimes. He had to push back—push through—until Jake talked to him. Now that he knew, he was confident he could do it.

"No," Jake mumbled. "And I'm okay with it, usually. I knew going into it that all this stuff would be a problem. But I just… wasn't ready. For anything that's happened. It's all… not on my terms."

Tristan rocked Jake gently and buried his nose in Jake's hair. "I know. It's all so fast."

"It's everything I want, but it's all *right now*, not… having time to grow into it. Not having a choice. Even if that's what I'd choose, if I *did* have one. Is that weird?" Jake asked, finally looking at him. He looked anxious about the answer.

"No, hon—baby," Tristan assured him. "Not at all."

Jake chuckled grimly. "And about that… I probably owe you an explanation."

"Not if you're not ready," Tristan said. It was a strange quirk, but there were plenty of possible reasons. It wasn't his place to question Jake only liking some pet names.

"I want to, though." Jake's voice was thick. "Now that I'm talking to you about everything."

"Of course. Shoot," Tristan told him, tracing his fingers along Jake's arm.

"My parents used to call me *honey* and *sugar* and *sweetie* when they wanted to be obnoxious. When I was arguing too much, or insisting I was a boy, or they just wanted to shut me up, they'd go super girly on me. They knew I'd shut up—and shut down."

"That's..." Tristan was speechless for a moment. "That's just fucking awful. I'm glad you left," he finally said, when he could form words.

All of a sudden, his own parents seemed less like cartoon villains in comparison. Sure, they'd told him he was making a mistake, but they hadn't told him to leave. Exactly the opposite—they'd told him to stay, and not run away.

It was time he told Jake about them, and he did, tentatively.

"They weren't acting hateful like yours. They just thought I was being a dumbass and throwing away a good future. And I didn't like hearing it, so I left. Which..." he trailed off.

Shit. It was the same kind of blow to his ego and confidence as a failed audition.

This was a pattern.

"Hm?" Jake prompted, looking up at him at last.

"I guess I just can't handle rejection," Tristan said slowly, now that he was backed into a corner. His cheeks burned, and he kind of wanted to disappear. "That's so... childish."

Jake rubbed his back. "We all have little childish things,

from *being* children and being shot down. I'm only praying we—I—can keep those to a minimum with our kid."

"Do you think I should get back in touch?" Tristan asked. "Now of all times, when we're having a kid, I'm starting to think about… wanting to broaden my family."

"Do you feel *obligated* to, or do you *want* to?"

Tristan sucked in a breath through his teeth and then laughed. "That's my boyfriend. Asking the smart questions." God, he'd chosen right. "I want to. I don't do shit because I feel obligated."

"Except look after me," Jake pointed out, his lips curving into a little teasing smile.

Tristan rolled his eyes but grinned. Jake wasn't the only one feeling like someone knew him all too well, and all too suddenly. "Fine. But it's not like you're a burden. It's the right thing to do, but I'd do it if you were just a friend."

"Let me move in with you?" Jake blinked. "Marry me, for the damn healthcare?"

Tristan nodded. "Sure. If you were in need and I could help… it would be wrong *not* to help."

"You know, I could just believe you." Jake breathily chuckled, and he finally leaned over to kiss him. "You're too good a man."

Tristan sure didn't believe *that*. He just chuckled and shook his head. "You make me want to be."

"Now, how about those cuddles?" Jake flopped onto the pillows and gazed up at him. "To celebrate my officially moving in?"

There was an offer Tristan couldn't resist. Not that he could ever resist Jake, even without those eyes at work.

And he didn't even want to try.

CHAPTER
Twenty-One

JAKE

THANK GOD THE MORNING SICKNESS WAS WEARING OFF.

Jake could get up before noon some days now, and he could even eat toast now. Too many days for the last few weeks, it had felt like he would never be able to stomach food again. But here he was, at ten in the morning, out of bed and eating toast. Almost like a normal person.

The bedrest enforced by the constant nausea was far more unbearable than the fact he'd lost his figure. His abs were long-gone, and his stomach was starting to round out now. His pecs were fading, too, since he'd been strictly avoiding heavy lifting.

The stakes were too high for him to worry about his vanity. But lying around doing nothing? That was driving him out of his mind.

"Hey, Kyle." Jake tried not to chew his nails when Kyle answered his phone with a chirpy greeting. "It's Jake."

"Hi! How's it going?"

"Well, um… I was wondering…" Jake double-checked that

it was a Saturday. God, who was he turning into? He didn't know anymore. "Are you off work today? And free?"

"Sure. Nic and I don't have plans. Do you need anything?"

"Um… I need to get clothes. I'm down to about two things that fit me," Jake admitted. His bank account wasn't doing great, but since he'd given up the rent and bills of his old place, he'd at least lost money much slower.

"Shopping trip? Nico and I love those!" Kyle enthused.

Jake chuckled. "That's why I thought of you guys." They were always well-dressed, in downright cool clothes. Often a lot more femme clothes than he was comfortable wearing, but meant they might know where to go that he could actually try on clothes before he bought them.

If he walked into a maternity wear store, he was pretty sure he'd get laughed out… at best.

"We'll pick you up," Kyle said. "It's a date. How about Tristan?"

"He's at work." Jake tried not to sound half as lonely or desperate for company as he felt. "Until at least eight, he figures. Probably later."

"Oh, man. He's been working so much! Zeph said he can never get through to him anymore. We were going to go out for lunch. Do you know when he's free?"

"He keeps his phone off whenever he's at work. If you tell me the date, I'll check in with him later." Jake made a note of it and left it on the counter, since he didn't trust his brain to remind him of anything anymore.

Before he knew it, Kyle promised to pick him up in an hour, and he had some social contact to look forward to. Or dread. God, he hardly remembered how to act in public anymore. A few weeks of isolation—especially of unemployment—felt like far longer.

At least Jake's belly was still so small that it just looked like a little extra weight on him. He wasn't sure when he was going to cross that tipping point into *obviously pregnant*, but he hoped it lasted as long as possible. The last thing he wanted was strangers to clock him while he was walking down the street. Not because of what they might say or think, but because of what they might do.

It's not backwoods Kansas anymore, he reminded himself as he changed into his other, slightly less ratty, sweatpants and a loose t-shirt. It wasn't classy, but it would have to do.

He hated relying on others, but until early afternoon, he didn't trust his body not to just catch a whiff of a food smell and reject everything in his stomach while he was driving. He'd very nearly had an incident while driving past McDonald's last week.

The doorbell rang just as Jake finished tidying his hair into something presentable. God, he was going to have to get a haircut before he started showing, too.

"Hi, darling!" Kyle swept him into a hug, and not for the first time, Jake found himself overwhelmed with gratitude that his boyfriend had picked such great friends, through Zeph.

Nic, who was always pleasant but much quieter, leaned around him to add his own wave and smile. "Hey."

"Hi, guys." He hugged them each in turn and grabbed his keys. Well, key.

It was strange to have just a key to his boyfriend's place on his keychain. Kind of like when—briefly, before the "privilege" was revoked for showing up with short hair—he'd had a single front door key to his parents' house hanging on the same rainbow heart-shaped keyfob. It was battered now after many apartments, but he still clung to it.

It was a reminder of his freedom.

"Ready to go?"

"Please," Jake said. God, was he ever.

Anywhere but at home.

"I just hate relying on him for everything," Jake said as he pushed hangers on the bar back and forth. "I'm not bringing anything into the household."

Kyle and Nic exchanged looks before Nic commented, "Except a baby. That's a job."

"I still want to try to do more. So if you know of any jobs going..."

He hadn't been able to focus on anything long enough to job hunt lately, but now that he was feeling better, he needed to get back to it. And find workplace-appropriate clothes, which was unlikely. He'd be lucky if he could find anything to wear that wasn't little better than a potato sack.

Kyle promised, "I'll keep an eye out. What about community college for skills?"

"Like the trades? If there's anything I can do, yeah." Practical skills like electrics and plumbing weren't his forte, but he'd give anything a try. "Like sewing something better than this shit."

Kyle cast him a thoughtful look. "You're joking, but... that's not a bad idea."

"I can barely sew a button on!"

"You can learn. If you're interested."

At this point, three rounds of fitting room hell later, Jake was starting to feel convinced he'd have to get interested pretty quickly, or stay in sweatpants for the next six months.

Hell, even if he'd been a woman, he didn't like the look of most of this stuff. It was all frilly and lace-covered, which delighted Kyle and Nic, but didn't fit his own style. Even the plain t-shirts had ruffles or ruching or whatever along the seams.

And then there were the jeans, which were so obviously cut for women that they'd look weird or press his packer into his junk until he went numb.

Overall, Jake had found four pieces that he was happy with, all of them the plainest garments he could get.

"I would wear this if I had boobs," he sighed as he put back the shirt and shrugged. "I'm done."

"Are you sure you don't need more?"

"Of course I need more!" Jake exclaimed, a little louder than he'd meant to. "But good luck actually finding anything. It's itchy or thin or hot, or it has this stupid shit." He batted at the ruffles and bows on some of the clothes nearby. "If I wanted to look sexy, I'd just get naked. Oh, wait. I'm not going to be sexy naked for, like, months. *Years.*" Now that he'd started, he couldn't seem to stop, and tears had welled up in his eyes.

"Jake, deep breaths." Kyle reached out to touch his arm, but Jake shook it off and paced back and forth.

Irrationally, Jake wanted to ignore all of his advice. He wanted so badly to just sit down and cry until someone figured out how to make a nice, professional shirt that fit him. Hell, he'd take a potato sack right now, as long as it didn't have awkward chest flaps for the boobs he didn't have.

These two had been so sweet about the whole thing that he felt bad snapping at them, but he couldn't keep his annoyance under wraps, either.

"It's the fucking hormones," he muttered under his

breath. Since starting testosterone, he'd felt so much more grounded. When he was angry, it was harder to keep it from clouding his common sense, but he didn't burst out crying like he had before.

Which meant people couldn't use that against him as his parents once had. And now he was vulnerable all over again.

It wasn't just embarrassing to get a harsh blast from the past—it rubbed in his face the fact that it had only just begun.

He was going to have to deal with life like this, always feeling like he was running on a tank that was just past empty, for months to come.

This time, it was Nic who rested his hand on his back. "Come on. Let's get outside and get some fresh air." The way they moved together—Kyle taking the hangers out of Jake's hands while Nic comforted him—made Jake ache for Tristan.

Jake didn't resist. He dug a couple wrinkled twenties out of his wallet and pressed them into Kyle's hand, then let Nic steer him out of the store.

"Sorry," Jake mumbled. His eyes stung as he wiped them again. He hadn't actually cried that much, but the frustration that had welled up inside him was so draining. "It's all... a lot to handle, at once. The baby, and losing my job, and moving in, and marriage..."

Shit. He hadn't meant to say that.

Nic's eyes got wide for a second. When he looked down at Jake, it was clearly toward his hand.

"Uh, we're not... telling anyone," Jake said, low and urgently. "Shit. Sorry. Can you keep that under wraps?"

Nic mimed locking his lips and throwing away the key. "But... why?"

"Health insurance."

Nic got it right away. "After getting fired, right? And his coverage is good?"

"Good enough for what we need." Jake patted his stomach lightly.

Nic nodded as he guided Jake to sit on the bench outside the store entrance. There was nobody hanging around outside, which made it easier to talk. "It's hard to find trans-friendly plans."

Though he wondered how Nic knew that, Jake nodded. "It is. It was a fight to get my top surgery approved. God, that feels like yesterday in some ways. And now I'm going back through the medical system. I hated my last surgeon. I swore I was done with doctors and all that shit. Except... this is what I want."

"I never wanted kids," Nic said. And, unless Jake was mistaken, his next words were, "Which is good. I had to get a hysto for bottom surgery." When Jake's head snapped up and he looked at him, Nic added, "Yeah, I'm stealth."

Everything made more sense all of a sudden: why Kyle had seemed so knowledgable, the stealth friend-of-a-friend Tristan had mentioned, and how considerate all the guys had been around him. Jake processed this for a few moments and nodded. "So you get the juggling act."

"Oh, yeah. Been there, done that." Nic patted his hand. "If you need a listening ear, I'm good at that."

Jake took a deep breath and tried to choose *what* he wanted to complain about. There were so many possibilities. "Everything's happened so fast. I've always wanted to have a kid or two of my own, but I was hoping for... later this year, or next year."

Nic whistled under his breath. "That's sudden."

"Yeah. I'd only just come off T, like, a couple months

before. I thought it would take a lot longer after so many years."

Nic nodded. "They do always obsessively tell us *T isn't birth control*, but… it kinda is."

Jake nodded back, glad to have someone around he could dump this on. "Until it's not. So it's what I want, but so fast. Same with Tristan. He's everything I could ever want in a guy, but he's here *now*, when the rest of my life is in chaos. Switching careers… I mean, that assumes I'm gonna find another career, but I've been forced into this. And handed an opportunity, if I can study or train or something over the next six months. But it's all now, now, now."

"And you haven't had time to decide," Nic said.

"Exactly. But I don't know why I feel like I need to do that." Jake folded his arms as he gazed toward the store entrance, waiting for Kyle to come out. "It *is* what I want. Shouldn't I be happy about everything?"

Nic seemed to be choosing his words carefully. "Sometimes we're good at fighting things we really want, just because we're so used to having to fight for everything we have. But things can go wrong, in all the right ways. And you can stumble into things you never expected. Usually at exactly the wrong time, but you *make* it the right time if you want it that bad."

Kyle emerged and looked around for them, and Nic stood up and waved him over. The smile on his face was precious —all the more so now that Jake knew that they had more in common than he'd thought.

I could have that, too.

"How are you doing?" Kyle asked when he reached them and handed over the bag and change.

The fresh air—as cool and fresh as L.A. smog ever got,

anyway—had done him a world of good. Jake straightened his shoulders and smiled up at him. "I'm ready to head home and nap that one off. Thank you, guys."

Hopefully they who can keep a secret.

Nic winked when Jake looked at him, as if guessing what he was thinking. With that much reassurance, Jake relaxed. Nic was right: it was time to trust the way his life was unfolding.

It might be imperfect, but it was *his* life, and he only got one chance at it.

CHAPTER
Twenty~Two
TRISTAN

"I LIKE THE CHEMISTRY BETWEEN YOU TWO. YOU HAVE A REAL intensity that's going to come out perfectly on screen. The screen tests didn't lie."

Tristan snapped back to reality and shook his head slightly to clear his thoughts. For a second, he'd wondered how the hell Stefan, the director, had known about him and Jake.

It was hard not to get distracted by his boyfriend—legally, his husband—when he was drawing so heavily on their relationship for his craft.

Brian's pride was evident as he jumped in to answer. "Tristan and I are planning on going over the sides for tomorrow before we leave."

"Yeah," Tristan chimed in. "It's helped a lot so far." They'd just run through their first blocking, and Stefan had been open to the ideas that he and Brian had thrown at him. That was promising in terms of their working relationship over the next few months.

As usual in the film industry, the first scene they were

shooting wasn't the first scene of the movie. By this point, they'd already met and become friends, and they were talking behind a tree, supposedly nearby a house party. But the party itself would be shot later this month. They were starting with some of the one-on-one outdoor scenes, making it a little easier to arrange filming as they finalized shooting locations for the indoor scenes.

It was a risky move to start with their first kiss, but it also made sense in terms of the overall storyboard. It wasn't Tristan's job to question it—he and Brian just had to make it work.

He liked Brian already, which made it easier. They'd talked a lot over the last few days about their characters and how they were going to play the emotional elements of this scene, so Tristan was glad but not surprised that Stefan was so pleased. He'd felt that chemistry himself.

"One thing, though." Stefan glanced between them. "Tristan, I think your portrayal is slipping a little too much into stereotypes. Can we reevaluate it together and come up with something more… well, more relatable?"

Tristan raised his eyebrow. He was starting to wonder what the hell these directors were smoking. "Am I being too gay for a gay movie?"

Brian laughed, but it was uncomfortable. In Tristan's eye, Brian's character, a young twenty-something who had been accepted by all his friends and family, was the harder one to play. At least his own character background had more meat to it—a compelling backstory of mixed acceptance and rejection that he could draw on.

And a very gay narrative, apparently.

"Oh, I wouldn't say that." Stefan chuckled uncomfortably.

"I like Brian's All-American attitude. I think the audience will relate to him, but you…"

Tristan stared him down, but Stefan kept talking.

"When we've blocked you moving, that… dramatic flair works well in the scene, but it will be more compelling if it's a divergence from how we see your character in other scenes."

Brian's gaze flickered between them both.

"So, tone down the camp from now on," Tristan interpreted. At best, this was heavyhanded direction. Actors didn't usually respond well to being told how to do their jobs, so he didn't feel bad acting peevish about it.

This so soon after the commercial? Why had everyone, all of a sudden, cast him in gay roles and then told him he was being too gay for the role?

Surely to God he wasn't suddenly acting noticeably gay now that he was in a gay relationship. It sounded like something a homophobe would say, and it didn't make sense even the moment he thought it, but the fear was still real.

Unless… There was one person who could shape the casting agents' and directors' impressions of him before he'd even met them. And Brian was straight—from everything he'd seen of him when he'd Googled him, he was the picture of perfect straightness. Wife and two kids and a square chin and loving parents and all.

It was an uncomfortable realization that maybe… just maybe… this sudden turnaround wasn't about the characters he played, but instead, it was based in something other than what he did on the clock. If Bobby had told directors his relationship business, he was going to be pissed off.

"No, no. We'll reevaluate as we go along, before we're… er… too invested in any single choice."

Tristan didn't like the sound of that at all. "I'll make the choices I feel fit the character best, because that's my job. I've read and reread the script at least as many times as you have over the last week." All the notes he'd made in the margins, and all the time he'd spent putting himself in that character's head—they weren't going to waste. "What sets our characters apart is our choices, and those are grounded in the script. I'll be as gay as the character demands. Brian's a lot like many of the gay guys I know. If you're not going to tell Brian to be less gay in a *gay movie*, don't try telling me that, either."

He stood and headed for his trailer. Technically *their* trailer—it wasn't a big-budget production, so he and Brian shared it.

And right now, he needed it more than Brian. Surely he had a few minutes to keep him from blowing his top. Stefan had to finish blocking and determining the camera positions before he and Brian were called back out. And he didn't want to be this pissed off when they actually shot the kiss scene.

He hadn't pulled a diva moment on set before, and it utterly terrified him to try it now, but he didn't see much choice. If he didn't put his foot down now, Stefan would try to dictate his choices to him. Not only would it piss him off, but it would ruin his own craft, and make it look like *his* choices. And maybe screw with the whole damn movie.

Tristan's confidence in his own choices was high. He—his character—didn't owe anyone an explanation for his mannerisms, and he wasn't going to apologize for it.

When real life and art collide.

Once he was alone in the trailer, he collapsed onto the couch and took deep breaths to calm himself down. Then, he dialed Bobby's number.

"Hey, kid." Bobby sounded surprised. "You on set today?"

"Yeah. They told me to dial down the gay… again. My character isn't going to apologize, and neither am I."

"Oh. Oh, yeah. I figured this might be a problem," Bobby said slowly. "You're handling it well, though? Do I need to come there?"

"Did you tell the directors I'm gay?"

There was a long pause, during which Tristan's heart sank. He hadn't expected this man of all people to let him down so completely.

"Bobby?"

Finally, Bobby answered. "I never said you were, in so many words."

Nobody knew better than Tristan that there were all kinds of ways to say something without words. He scoffed. "Yeah, but you've let them believe it. So you can cast me easier in roles."

"You've gotten more work lately than you did for—what, six months before? And this is a big opportunity," Bobby told him. He sounded strangely defensive. Like he was feeling guilty.

"You still had no right to make my private business part of my job," Tristan hissed. Then, he paused. "When did you start telling people?"

Again, no answer.

"Is that why I wasn't getting bookings last year? Because you took that risk for me, and it didn't pay off? So then your only choice was to submit me for gay roles and play on my *natural strengths*? Does everyone already know?"

Nothing.

"Bobby?" Tristan's voice rose. "Does everyone already know about me?"

"Look. It's a dog-eat-dog world in Hollywood. They gotta know what box to put you in. They've got an idea of what they want, and if you fit that stereotype, they don't have to imagine—"

"An actor doing his damn job? They don't have to imagine me pretending to be someone I'm not, as if I'm not already doing that?" Tristan was hot under the collar. He'd never argued with Bobby this seriously, but it felt like all his trust had been swept away.

Like the blindfold had been ripped off, or maybe the bandaid, because the betrayal ached.

"I'm not gonna defend this to you now," Bobby told him. "I did what I thought was right."

Tristan scoffed. "I can't trust you, man. All this time, I was trying to keep it under wraps because that's what I thought you wanted me to do. You know how my personal life suffered? All the fear of... of, hell, being seen out with my best friend at gay clubs?"

"And I did want you not to flaunt it. And I still do," Bobby told him, his voice rising. "It's like jumping through the eye of a needle to make this work, Tris. You can't be *openly* gay for this to work. Or you'll be stuck doing indie shit for the rest of your life. You gotta be just gay enough to get the role, but straight enough that you get awards for it."

The harsh truth stung. Tristan opened and closed his mouth a few times, and then pressed the heel of his hand into his forehead. "Things are changing."

"No, they're not. Go do your damn job and let me finish doing mine."

Just then, the trailer door opened, so Tristan hit the "end call" button. God, he wished telephones still had receivers so he could slam it down. Cutting it off didn't seem like enough of a *fuck you* right now.

It was Brian. Though Tristan tried for a smile, it felt fake.

"Hey, man." Brian came to sit next to him and punched his shoulder in an equally forced display of cheer. "I hate to tell you, but we might only have a couple minutes." He spoke low and urgently now. "I overheard Stefan saying something that sounded kinda like he's looking at… at replacing you."

Tristan couldn't feel his fingers for a few moments. His heartbeat pounded in his ears. "Because of what I said?" Sure, there were protections, but those didn't keep him fully safe. Actors got replaced over creative differences all the time.

"I don't know. He wants me to talk to him in a minute. I don't think he meant me to overhear what I did." Brian didn't sound apologetic about it, though. Had he been deliberately listening in?

Tristan rubbed his face and sighed. "Thanks for telling me. Apparently my agent's been spreading stories about me. God knows what Stefan thinks of me."

"You got anything else lined up after this?"

Tristan snorted. It would be dumb to try scheduling anything too soon after a production of this size. If production ran late, he'd have to pull out of the other one. "Not yet. My agent wanted this to be my big break. Once production's well and truly underway, he can use Stefan's name to shop me around."

"Yeah." Brian shook his head. "It would be a dick move to pull you at this stage. Career-wise, money-wise."

God, that was right. "I can't afford to lose this," Tristan murmured, rubbing his cheeks and bracing his elbows on his knees. "Not with a baby on the way, when I'm the only one of us working." Jake had never specifically asked for his support, but that was typical of him. Tristan only wanted all the more to offer him that support and take one big worry off Jake's mind.

Getting fired after a week on set would not ease Jake's mind and stress.

Brian sucked in a breath, not answering for a few moments. Then, he squeezed his shoulder. "Yeah. I've been there. Look, let me talk to him, man. I'll be back in a bit."

Like that, he was gone, and Tristan was left to decide how much of his art he was willing to sell out in the name of responsibility.

God, responsibility sucked.

He didn't have long to think before there was a knock on the trailer door. Stefan came in and shut the door. "Can we talk?"

So soon? That was a fucking quick decision. My replacement must have jumped on the chance. "Sure."

"I have to apologize for meddling so much with your choices. I was making a knee-jerk judgment at way too early a stage to do that," Stefan told him, shaking his head and offering a hand to shake. "I don't want bad feelings."

It felt like a trick somehow, but Tristan slowly reached out to take his hand. "No hard feelings, I guess." *As long as this doesn't happen again,* he thought, but he didn't have to say it.

"You're doing a stellar job. Everyone's impressed with how well you're embodying your character. Keep it up." Stefan stood up and nodded. "We're nearly ready. You've got five minutes to go over the scene again."

Tristan could have recited both of their dialogue from memory—there wasn't much. It was mostly nonverbal, and he remembered the blocking perfectly well. "Yeah. Thanks," he said anyway. He needed the time to figure out what had just happened.

"Congratulations on the baby, by the way." Stefan grinned and clapped his shoulder, and then moved for the trailer door.

Tristan was left staring after Stefan, his discomfort only growing. *What the hell was that all about?* He shook his head and collapsed back against the couch.

Had he used a pronoun when talking about the pregnancy to Brian? It was just a few minutes ago, but he was pretty sure he hadn't. Brian had assumed he was straight and gone to Stefan, who now thought he was the bee's knees for playing gay.

In the weirdest way possible, after all his tentative steps out of the closet, he was right back in it. And since he was determined not to compromise his own acting just to play a more "relatable" character, if he wanted to take care of Jake, he had a hell of a hard choice to make.

And he couldn't make it without asking Jake, which meant placing more stress on him than Tristan wanted in a new relationship. But he also couldn't very well tell anyone he had a pregnant boyfriend without making sure Jake was okay with that. And similarly, he couldn't avoid talking about his own personal life for weeks to come without making sure Jake was fine with being hidden away.

More complications. Great. That's the last thing I need.

Twenty~Three

JAKE

WAS HIS DISTRESS THAT EASY TO SENSE? OR HAD NIC AND Kyle texted Tristan? Either way, Jake didn't care.

The important part was that they were kissing. In fact, the moment Tristan had walked through the door, he grabbed Jake around the waist and kissed him like he'd been gone for months.

Jake melted into Tristan's arms, breaking the kiss only to bury his nose in Tristan's shoulder and inhale the scent of him. It was amazing how much that alone could relax him. He swayed willingly when Tristan rocked him side to side. "Welcome home," he murmured.

As always, Tristan had something simple and sweet and romantic to say to him. "It's easy to look forward to getting home to you."

"Did Kyle and Nic give you a heads-up?"

"About what? No." Tristan pulled back, trying to look at him.

Jake didn't let him just yet, because he wasn't ready to let go. Those strong arms around his shoulders did everything to boost his mood after a long, tiring day alone with his own thoughts.

"It's no big deal," Jake assured him. "I just had a shitty day clothes shopping."

Tristan squeezed him, and when he pulled away again, Jake let him. "I'm sorry, baby."

Jake shrugged it off, more concerned about Tristan's need for contact. "It happens. What about you?" He guided Tristan to the table for supper, giving him some time to calm down as he listened to Tristan's day. He could tell Tristan was holding something back, but he'd get around to it.

Eventually, after supper, it came out. Tristan sighed and deflated as they moved to the couch together. "I need to ask you something."

Jake tensed up. Those words were rarely good.

"If it came down to it, how would you feel about me telling people I have a boyfriend, and that you're pregnant?"

Jake almost wasn't sure he'd heard the question correctly at first. "Coming out? All the way out?"

"I guess I should ask: do you *want* me to?"

This was a different question completely. Jake spotted the difference easily: one was Tristan asking permission, and the other was Tristan seeing if Jake wanted him to do it.

They'd talked about it enough damn times that Tristan ought to have known his answer. "If you're ready to come out, then do it. If you're not... we'll make it work for now." That last part was important, because Jake didn't want to feel like a secret forever.

Tristan sighed. "I've told them there's a baby on the way. I think it saved my job. But now I feel like shit, because..." he trailed off, casting Jake a guilty look.

"You didn't say I'm a he," Jake surmised. Anxiety tightened his chest. Practically speaking, the first thing he ought to be worrying about was *it saved my job*. But his heart wasn't in that question. Not as much as the other one he wanted to ask. "I've been out for years. Plenty of people know. But you're coming out as gay, and then as a partner of a trans person—which isn't like coming out *as* trans, but people can be weird. Are you willing to deal with the reactions if you tell them?"

"I don't know. If I lose my job, no." Tristan took his hands. "I know you hate feeling like I'm supporting you, but I want to. Right now, I can, if I keep this role."

"Keep this role?" Jake asked. He was at least relieved that Tristan knew how hard it was on him to accept help, and Tristan still kept trying to support him anyway. "Lose your job?"

It didn't make sense. He knew how hard Tristan had worked lately—if not on set, he was staying up until all hours rehearsing. Jake had fallen asleep several times to the halting rhythm of murmured words from the living room: Tristan learning his lines.

Then, it hit Jake: was *he* the problem? "Because you're gay, or because you're with me?"

Tristan shook his head. "Neither? Both? I don't know." His distress was hard to witness, and Jake slid his arms around him as he listened. "I shot the big kiss scene today. Apparently I was too camp, until they thought I was straight, and now I'm doing a wonderful job playing outside my life experience," he said drily. "Bobby's outed me to people. I don't know how many, and he won't tell me. So that's why work's been slow lately. And why he's submitting me to so many gay roles. He told me he wanted me to be a big-shot straight actor who gets awards for playing gay. I thought I wanted that for ages. I don't want that life now, but I wish I'd had the choice myself."

Jake sighed and held his boyfriend tight. "I'm sorry. He's been outing you?"

"As good as. He said he's never *told* anyone, exactly, but… suddenly, I've been in all these camp movies? And even when I'm playing a serious role like this, I'm too camp?"

"Sure." Jake snorted. "People are weird."

"I feel like I'm being bounced around between boxes. Too gay for this, too straight for that. Where the fuck is my box?" Tristan rested his head on Jake's shoulder. "And more importantly, what happens if I lose this job?"

Jake kissed Tristan's temple. "I'll find work if I need to. I'm over the first trimester. My morning sickness is done. I can get away with my belly for the second trimester. And I'm looking at starting a business. If we have to move somewhere cheaper, that's okay."

Tristan looked over at him, and the resolve in his eyes startled Jake. "No. I've been trying to run away when the going gets hard for too long. I'll get work—if I have to get another agent, I don't care. I'll audition every day. I might not be around as much as I'd like to help you out, but I'm going to make it, whatever those assholes have to say about it. And I'm gonna make sure that, even if you do get a job or business of your own, you don't *need* to struggle to make ends meet."

The air rushed out of Jake all at once. From anyone else, he might not have believed it, but Tristan had been by his side for even longer than Jake had been willing to let him be.

Tristan was willing to stay closeted, even when his whole life had been building to this moment of finally being himself, just so he could protect Jake. Not socially, but financially and emotionally and in a very real physical sense.

He'd already given Jake so much, and he wanted to give him more? To continue to walk the line and stay in the shadows, just so Jake was safe and comfortable?

Jake welled up and pressed his forehead into Tristan's shoulder. "I'm mad they're making you make that choice," he murmured when he could manage to speak again. "But I'm... I'm just..." He was almost speechless at both the fact that Tristan wanted to be there for him, and that he wanted to let him. "Thank you."

How could he return that support? The answer was obvious: by being here for him right now, when he was struggling with his own dilemma.

"Anything for you, baby." Tristan's voice had that shy, almost fearful quality. "I just want... you to be happy. And the baby, of course. But you're my number one concern."

Jake had to come out and say it. "All this time, I've been worrying about our relationship. That it was just hot sex that turned into pregnancy and you're just doing the right thing by me. It was hard to believe that you actually love me."

Tristan sucked in his breath, his alarm visible.

"There's nothing more you could have done," Jake added with a little half-smile. "That's my damage." In the safety of Tristan's arms, he could talk about it. "My parents... you know they threw me out, huh? But I think it was a convenient excuse. They weren't happy together. They pretty much got married because of me. And the last thing I want to do..." he trailed off, choking up.

"Is make the same mistake," Tristan whispered. "God, h— baby. I'm sorry about all of that."

"You can call me honey, too, if you want. And anything

they used to call me. I don't want them to have power over all those words," Jake admitted. His voice was shaky, but he was certain of what he said. "I'm a hot hormonal mess, but I know what I feel, and I love you. And you married me, just to help me out when you could have walked away... and you're having to deal with all my shit, and all of your own..."

Tristan held a finger over his lips, his smile gentle and sincere. "No. I married the man I could see myself marrying anyway," he told Jake. "The kind of man who can deal with the wrong hormones flooding his brain, and birth a kid at the end of all of this, and have everyone around him telling him who he really is because of it? That's a hell of a guy. And everything I've learned about you has only made me more sure that my gut instinct was right about you. Baby aside, I knew I loved you before then. I just wasn't ready to admit it to either of us."

Jake was tearing up again. God, all this crying was getting exhausting. "Really?"

"Really," Tristan chuckled gently. "You captivated me from the very beginning."

Jake finally pulled away and wiped his eyes so he could look at Tristan. "Do you believe in love at first sight?"

"Yes and no," Tristan answered after a moment's thought. "See, in the movie I'm doing, it's supposed to be—and then then it all goes wrong, and it gets put back together again. And it's been dramatized for the screen, but I think a lot of relationships are like that. You choose a person, and then you *make* it work."

A shiver ran down Jake's spine. He rarely heard anyone say something that rang so true to him. "Yeah. It's not magic. The spark is, but you can have a spark with lots of different people."

"But only that one in a million kind of guy will make you stop and question everything," Tristan said, nodding. "A spark is great. But we've always had a fire. I wanted to get to know you, and I've never been disappointed."

Again, Jake pressed his forehead into Tristan's shoulder as Tristan rubbed his back. "Me, neither. I kept holding my breath and waiting for you to… to leave, or to kick me out, I guess. I was afraid of relying on you and giving you that power over me. But… it's not like that. My parents issued ultimatums. *Do this or get out,* you know? You've been… welcoming me in."

Tristan shook his head. "Trying, anyway. I know you've had to sacrifice to be with me, too. And I might have to ask you to keep doing that, until I can safely be me. Or to ride through it with me, if I do come out and it doesn't go well. I wish I had more to offer, but… I've only got me."

"That's all I want," Jake whispered, pressing kisses against Tristan's lips until Tristan's expression relaxed and he seemed to really believe it.

"We're both vulnerable with each other. You've got my heart, baby," Tristan whispered.

Jake smiled. "And I want to take care of it every bit as much as you do."

"Let's be careful with each other's hearts, then," Tristan murmured, pulling back to cup his cheeks. "And keep talking, and… figure this out one step at a time. It's scary, but if we're together…"

"If we're together," Jake finished, "we'll be okay."

"Yeah," Tristan murmured. "We'll be okay."

CHAPTER

Twenty~Four

TRISTAN, TWO WEEKS LATER

FOR THE FIRST WEEK, IT WAS EASY TO BE GRATEFUL HE STILL had a job. Tristan suspected Brian had gotten involved and refused to work with a replacement actor, since Brian refused to confirm or deny it when he'd asked him point-blank.

He'd played it cool both on and off-set with his coworkers, never talking much about his personal life since that one slip with Brian. Despite Jake's support of whatever he decided to do, he wanted to feel like he was more stable before he came out.

But his conversations with Bobby kept replaying in his head. If he kept him as an agent, he was buying into that bullshit and letting him build him a career based on strategic lies. Bobby wasn't seeing that he couldn't live life the way he had for the past five years. Coming out was inevitable. No matter when he did it, if it would tank his career, it wouldn't matter when he did it.

Might as well get it over with now, and if he lost work, at least he wouldn't have to lose a piece of his soul every time

204

the rest of the cast talked about their relationships and he had to bite his tongue.

Not to mention, if he did lose his career, better to do that sooner and stop missing out on important moments—like Jake's first ultrasound today. What else he could do, he had no idea, but he could worry about that later.

He broke the speed limit more than once on his way home, he was so eager to hear how it had gone.

By the time he burst inside, Jake was waiting for him with supper—as usual, these days—and the sight warmed his heart. He'd never expected Jake to work so hard to help him out, but it made sense. Jake wasn't the kind of guy to laze around just because he had the chance. Another little reason he loved him, even if Jake would just get confused or flustered if he ever told him.

"Hey, babe," Jake greeted.

Tristan strode over to him and beamed. "Hey, gorgeous." Jake was looking healthier these days, too—he'd put on baby weight, and it suited him. He didn't look so much like he was skipping meals and stressing about everything. The glow suited him. "Tell me everything!"

Jake led him to the table, and over supper, he got the details.

The ultrasound had gone well. No signs of problems so far, and the chances of something going wrong were dropping with every week that passed.

"So nothing more we need to do?" Tristan wanted to make sure Jake had everything he needed, even if insurance didn't cover it. He expected another confused phone call tomorrow from the insurance company.

Jake shook his head. "I'll just keep eating my spinach."

"Good man," Tristan grinned. The books on the side table

finally caught his eye—they were new. "What's that about?" he asked as he gestured with his fork.

"Oh." Jake looked sheepish. "Um, medical stuff."

"For you, or for a job?" He wasn't blind. He might work long hours, but in the precious time they did have together, he'd seen Jake looking at job sites again. Medical coding, most recently.

Jake chuckled. "Both. If I can make a difference and help out… and get a job without having to invest in starting it up…" he shrugged, but he looked half-hearted about it. Tristan could read Jake's expression quicker than any of those books, and that spark wasn't there.

"Is that what you really want to do?" Tristan asked. "I know you liked science, but is this something you feel good about?"

Jake blinked and squinted at him. "How did you know that about me?"

"Science fair."

It took Jake a few moments to remember. Then, he set down his fork and stared. "I told you that the first time we hooked up." His tone was awed.

Tristan blushed and looked at his plate. "Yeah, well. I've always paid attention to the things you've said." As far as he was concerned, that was the minimum possible bar he could have stepped over in a relationship.

Jake's voice was soft. "I appreciate that." He cleared his throat, and after a moment, he changed the subject enough that Tristan looked back up again. "No, I don't love it. But do you love your job? You've told me before how torn you are, but you're still willing to do it. Part of growing up—into the kind of person who can sustain a relationship—is being willing to do the things you don't want to, if the other person needs it. And if I can have a job that helps give you a little more freedom of choice…"

Oof. Tristan hadn't expected that. Again, as with everything Jake did, it made sense, but it came out of the blue. This man never stopped surprising him with the size of his heart. "I love you for wanting to give me that choice," he admitted. "Wow."

"Least I can do," Jake said with a chuckle. "For my husband." Then, he blushed and looked down at his plate.

Tristan paused and stared at him. It was rare that either of them brought that up. Why now? He cleared his throat to catch his eye again. "Babe. I think we're at an impasse. We're both willing to sacrifice for the other person, but neither of us wants to accept that help. And both of us have to learn that, if we want to make this work."

Jake laughed. "Yeah."

"For my part," Tristan led, drawing a deep breath, "I hate missing things like the ultrasound today. And I'm going to miss so much more, if I keep on this path. It's really hard to resolve that in my head. I'll have months where you get sick of seeing me around, and then months where you never see me. And with a newborn… I'll miss once-in-a-lifetime moments." It was the first time he'd admitted even to himself how much that worried him.

"Are you getting cold feet now that you're settled in this job?" Jake asked. His tone wasn't judgmental, but the words themselves stung.

More than that, it was true—he'd kept his head down and prayed to keep the role. Stefan hadn't replaced him, though, and he hadn't been meddling with Tristan's choices. They were far enough into production now that Tristan felt like he was safe.

And now that he was safe, he had the itch to throw himself into danger once again.

"I… yeah," Tristan admitted quietly, once he'd swallowed the honest truth. He loved that Jake gave it to him—in every possible way—but sometimes, like now, it hurt. "My ego. Again with the fear of rejection. But I feel stupid saying that. I can't afford to have an ego right now."

"Honey," Jake said, setting down his fork and leaning over to take his hand. "You're good enough to get hired no matter who you're screwing… or even married to. If you want to leave acting, then do it. If you want to keep acting, commit to it. After this movie, take some time to figure out which it'll be, but don't keep waffling back and forth."

Again, it stung, but it was too true. He'd been so indecisive for so long about whether he wanted to pursue this that he hadn't made any real effort either way. Sure, he'd promised himself he'd audition more and hit the streets to knock on doors, but he hadn't followed through.

And he was afraid that if he came out and Hollywood rejected him, like Bobby thought would happen, it would crush his heart.

"And missing moments happens. It'll happen no matter what job either of us does," Jake added when Tristan didn't say anything. "A lot of actors are married with kids. They make it work. So what's really worrying you?"

Tristan slowly shook his head as he chuckled. "You oughta be an actor yourself. You've got a way of getting to the truth." And that, he realized, was exactly it. "I… Everything I'm doing in this movie?" Jake's encouraging nod gave him the confidence to continue. "I feel like it's too personal. My heart's in this, and I'm way more vulnerable on screen. Actors always are, because we're putting out feelings out there. And now it's a gay story, and there's romance, and… every time I look at him and the cameras are rolling, I imagine he's you. Except his character has a bunch of friends and family supporting him. But you didn't, and you still made it. You're tough as fucking nails, baby."

Jake laughed sheepishly, but he didn't deny it. "Are you proud of what you do?"

It was a good question. Tristan had to take a moment to think about it. He was now, and he was especially proud of doing it without letting anyone tell him how. "Yeah. Yeah, I am. I'm ready to be proud of who I am, too. No more hiding on set. No more letting Bobby tell me who I need to be to stay employed. It's not gonna be easy, but…"

"But I promised to be there with you," Jake said. "And I meant it. I so appreciate that you want to keep me safe, but you need to be happy. And hiding me… for some reason, doesn't make you happy."

If Jake kept this up, maybe one day, Tristan would feel like he was worth all that love he heard in Jake's voice. "Of course not. I don't want to hide the best thing that ever happened to me," he told Jake, and that smile made his heart absolutely melt.

"What do you expect on set?"

Tristan nodded. "It'll be fine. I mean, we're doing a gay movie, for God's sake. People won't care. I've been using the long-term picture as an excuse."

"I don't want to let you use excuses anymore," Jake told him with a frank smile. "You're better than that."

Tristan beamed. The only other guy he trusted to do that was Zeph, and he was the best friend a guy could ask for. He couldn't think of a better trait to have in a partner. "Thank you. I'll commit, then," Tristan said, drawing a deep breath.

"For real this time. If Bobby doesn't like it, I'll fire him. I'll tell the world who I am, and I'll audition for everything I can." He was fired up now—more so than he could remember being in a long time. "I don't want to hold myself back and give myself excuses if I fail. If I've tried my hardest and it doesn't work, I'll deal with it then. But maybe it won't go terribly. Times are changing, whatever Bobby says."

"They are," Jake said with a smile. "Gay actors? Pregnant men? What's next? People minding their own business?"

Tristan laughed. "Oh, I wish."

He was still smiling as he finished his dinner and cleared away the dishes, and as he and Jake headed to the bedroom afterward.

Every time he and Jake talked, it felt like another brick being laid in the foundation of their relationship. One more reason to trust that it would all work out. Without Jake at his side, he might have had less need to make money, sure. But he never would have had the guts to be himself no matter what, either.

A guy couldn't get much luckier.

CHAPTER
Twenty~Five
JAKE

TRISTAN WOULD HAVE TORN THIS LOCUM OBSTETRICIAN A NEW one. Jake would have, too, if he'd been expecting it.

But nobody had bothered giving him a heads-up that his usual doctor was on vacation, and apparently, nobody had told *him* that he'd be seeing a pregnant man, either.

Jake choked back the tears of frustration. If he'd only known, he could have prepared himself mentally, or brought more paperwork, or asked the trans-friendly doula to accompany him.

Instead, he was facing this alone, and the last six years of his life weighed on him.

"Is that everything for today?" Jake asked coldly. He didn't care if he came off as rude, but he didn't want this asshole seeing that he'd successfully gotten to him.

"You do know you can't breastfeed, right? Bottle-feeding is associated with poorer health outcomes, too." The disapproval, even scorn, in the doctor's voice was impossible to miss. They were months away from Jake needing to worry about it. The only possible reason he could be bringing it up was to make Jake feel inferior as a parent, and that was the last straw.

"Look," Jake said, standing up. "If you're not going to give me my fourteen-week checkup, just say so."

"I don't see where your problem is coming from," Dr. Whoever said. Williams, Jake thought he'd heard the receptionist say. Williams rolled his eyes. "Many women experience uncontrollable emotions…"

Jake had put up with quite enough of this for one day. He had no doubt this was the kind of guy who thought women were ruled by their uncontrollable emotions, and PMS made women crazy. Even after transition, Jake had no time for assholes who said that kind of shit.

He headed for the door. "There's no reason for me to put up with disrespect. Goodbye." The doctor tried to say something, but Jake tuned it out as he walked out of the office, shaking but glowing with pride.

His usual obstetrician would be back next week, the receptionist had said. He'd wait until then, and complain when he talked to her. She slipped on pronouns sometimes, or would say *women* and then look apologetic or confused. But she sure as hell didn't revel in it the way this guy had— deliberately sprinkling language throughout his sentences and looking at Jake's reactions.

Once he got to his car, Jake let the brave front drop and slumped back in his seat, crying it out.

It was the worst feeling in the world to be called something he wasn't, but he dealt with it when it was unavoidable or unintentional. Someone like this Williams guy deliberately baiting him was nothing he should have had to deal with. The afternoon stretched ahead of him, and then a long evening, and then part of the night, before he was going to see Tristan again.

Whatever he told Tristan so as not to upset him, Jake missed his presence sometimes. Having someone stare at him weirdly and call him *female* as much as humanly possible in one sentence was one of those times.

It was the middle of the day, but he called Nic before he knew what he was doing.

"Hey, Jake," Nic answered almost right away. "What's up?"

Jake sniffed and cleared his throat. "Um, are you or Kyle free today?"

"I can be," Nic told him. "What's up?"

Fuck. Now he had to actually *ask* for help, and Jake didn't know how to do that. "I… I just had a shitty obstetrician appointment. I kind of wanted company…" he trailed off.

"Where are you now?"

"The parking lot," Jake admitted with a shaky laugh.

"Oh, shit. You mean you just got out of it now?"

"I don't want to drive while I'm…" Jake trailed off, wiping his eyes again. "Sorry. God." He felt bad that Nic was seeing him such a mess again, but he'd never once judged him.

In the weeks since the Target incident, he'd seen one or the other of the guys more than once. They'd treated him exactly like normal, and he'd grown to realize that they really were that kind of person who wouldn't freak out and run away when he was his real self with them.

It was the kind of friendship he planned to hang onto.

"I was working from home anyway. I can take off for a couple hours. I'll be right there," Nic promised. "Text me the address."

"What? No, you don't have to come here."

"If you're upset, no driving," Nic said firmly. "Let me come there."

Jake let out a long breath. Nic was right. He wasn't going to put himself and everyone else at risk by doing something dumb for his pride's sake.

"Okay. Thank you."

"See you in a minute."

Jake pushed the sun visor down and reclined in his seat, folding his hands on his stomach as he waited for his friends. For once in his life, he didn't feel absolutely shitty about waiting to be rescued, either.

If there was one thing he'd learned over the last few months, it was that everyone needed help sometime. He couldn't wait until he could pay it forward.

***

"Hello," Nic greeted the receptionist with a sunny, yet firm smile. He had a *take no bullshit* attitude on, and she seemed to recognize that right away.

Jake tried not to cling to his side. Even being in here again gave him anxiety, but once Nic had heard what happened, he refused to let Jake leave without getting proper medical care. And he was right, but Jake hadn't been able to imagine walking back in here without someone like Tristan at his side.

Or, apparently, Nic, who was already explaining that Jake had cut an appointment short, and while they waited to file a complaint, Dr. Williams should see him again—this time, properly. And this time, accompanied by Nic as well as another representative from the medical clinic.

It took a little while, but eventually the clinic manager got involved. She first tried to insist that they couldn't have another appointment, but in polite but firm terms, Nic stood his ground.

Jake was too wrapped up in anxiety over the prospect of seeing Dr. Williams again to pay much attention to the back-and-forth until Nic looked at him.

"Is that okay? Seeing him again for a shorter appointment, with Sarah and me there?"

Jake nodded slowly, even if his heart raced. He'd had enough shitty doctors for one lifetime, and he didn't want more. But his own health was on the line, as was the baby's. He couldn't afford pride.

"Yes."

Before he knew it, they were whisked through into an examination room—a different one, this time—and Sarah went off without them.

Nic squeezed his hand. "Sure you're okay?"

Jake offered him a smile. "Terrified, but with witnesses, he might be better. Thank you." He couldn't thank Nic enough for showing up for him like this.

"My pleasure," Nic assured him. "It'll be over with before you know it. And next week, you can file that complaint. I'll come along for that if you want, too."

Jake's smile broadened. "It's nice to have friends. Especially ones who will kick ass for you."

"Yeah," Nic grinned back at him. "I do love kicking ass."

The door opened, and Dr. Williams entered, accompanied by Sarah. As Dr. Williams read his chart notes, he spoke in such a cursory manner that Jake might have taken offense. If he weren't so relieved that Dr. Williams was suddenly avoiding pronouns or gender references, he would have.

All you had to do last time was this, he mentally told the doctor, but he held it in for now and answered the questions.

One quick exam later, he was done. There weren't even any blood tests—not until his next appointment in two weeks' time, Dr. Williams explained.

"Thank you for your time," Nic said, unfailingly polite as he steered Jake out. Jake didn't even feel very bad not thanking Dr. Williams. He did smile and nod at Sarah on the way by, though.

Once they were outside, Nic high-fived him. "You did it."

"And it wasn't even that scary," Jake admitted with a laugh. "Sure, he acted like he was allergic to me, but…"

"Better than being an even bigger dickface about it. Now, celebratory French fries before I have to head back to work?"

Jake laughed. "Yes, please. I'd murder for some fries."

"I'll help you hide the body," Nic told him with a straight face. "Come on. I'll drive."

Twenty-Six

TRISTAN

TRISTAN HAD NO IDEA WHAT HAD COMPELLED HIM TO PICK UP his phone during lunch break, but for once, he actually checked it. The message waiting there made his gut drop.

I'm okay, but the gyn appointment today was with a locum and it went badly. Nic picked me up and advocated for me. Had a second appointment and all is well with me + baby though. Hope your day goes better!

"Fuck," he muttered under his breath, slowing down as he pushed his plate of catered food back.

"What's the matter?" He and Brian usually ate together, and his costar looked concerned for him.

Tristan shook his head. "My partner had a bad medical appointment today." Over the last couple weeks, he'd said *boyfriend* and *partner* in strategic conversations, and he was pretty sure most people had gotten the message now, but he and Brian had never really addressed it. "I wish I could be there for him more."

"Ahh. That's gotta be hard, man," Brian frowned. Then, he hesitated. "Can I ask you something?"

Tristan had been expecting it ages ago. "Yeah. He's my boyfriend, and he's pregnant."

"Oh." Brian took a few seconds to understand. "Right. Cool. That's… that question. You know, I told Stefan you had a pregnant girlfriend. Now he probably thinks you're in a three-way."

Tristan laughed. "I can barely handle a boyfriend. I don't know what I'd do with two partners."

"I feel you there," Brian agreed with a grin. "So, are you… um, public about all that? Or should I keep it hush-hush?"

"Starting to get there," Tristan shrugged. "This movie will be a big clue. I'll be open in interviews and stuff from now on." He bit his lip as he looked back at the phone. "But I don't care if it gets out. I've been too closeted for too long."

"Good for you, man," Brian said. "But yeah, it's hard when you can't be there. I've gone through it, too, with my wife."

"How do you deal with it?"

"Reminding myself that she wants me to do what makes me happy, and that we've all gotta work. I'm gonna miss those moments somehow. I might as well do something I'm proud of, and support them, and… make a difference. If movies like this break down stereotypes, and show people that straight actors can play gay… hopefully you guys start to get chances to play straight characters, too."

"That's what I'm counting on." Tristan shared a smile with Brian. At least that was one worry out of his hair. Now he had to figure out what to do about Jake.

It was going to be a long day before he could get home to him. For now, all he could do was send him a string of hearts and tell him how much he loved him.

"Oh, my God. You're home early!"

The surprise and joy on Jake's face was totally worth skipping drinks with the cast. Tristan didn't want to make a habit of it and screw with his attempts to make the set feel like a little family, but right now, he needed to be here. His real-life family came first.

Jake's reaction confirmed to him that it was the right thing to do.

"I'm here as soon as I could be," Tristan told him, and then he paused and stared around at Jake.

He had fabric draped everywhere, needles spread over the table, his sewing machine halfway taken apart, and printed instructions taped to the wall.

"Did I find Santa's workshop?"

Jake laughed as he danced through the mess and came to hug him. "Surprise: you married an elf."

"That explains how you're always so beautiful," Tristan murmured, pressing a kiss against Jake's lips. God, he loved seeing him blush, but he also loved knowing that he was telling Jake his feelings, and hopefully Jake felt good because of it.

"You flatterer," Jake giggled, rubbing his cheek against Tristan's shoulder.

"I'm sorry I couldn't be there today."

Jake shook his head. "It's honestly fine. I'm gonna submit a complaint next week, though… what's your schedule?"

"I'll make time," Tristan promised. He had no idea how, but he'd do anything to be at Jake's side when he stood up for himself. They didn't film seven days a week, either. As long as Jake was flexible on when that day was, he could make it work.

Making it work is our theme, isn't it? Speaking of which,

this was the second time Jake had said something Tristan kind of wanted to revisit. "Hey," Tristan said, letting Jake steer him to the bedroom, which seemed to be the only place safe from the fabric explosion. "You know, I told Brian about you today. And you know what the first thing I thought was?"

"What's that?"

"Reminding myself not to call you my husband." Tristan ran his hand down Jake's arm. "But then I felt bad about hiding that, like it's a secret. Like *you're* a secret. I don't want any part of this to be."

Jake's expression lit up, but then he seemed to consciously school his face. Like he was trying not to be too excited. "You don't think people will judge us for getting married already?"

"No way. If they do, fuck 'em." Tristan smiled at him. "We made a choice, and I'm so glad we did."

Jake pulled him in and ran his hand up Tristan's chest to cup his cheek. "I agree. It's not like we're worried about people judging anything else about us. Your friends might be surprised, but…"

"But happy," Tristan concluded. "I know they will be. And I'd be so, so happy if you'd let me call you by that title. I know it's just legal, and it was for the healthcare…"

"Oh, we both know that was only half-true," Jake said with a quiet chuckle. He flopped on his back on the bed. "I wouldn't have done that with any other guy. And whatever you say, you wouldn't have done that *for* just any guy."

"No," Tristan agreed after a few moments of thought. There was something different about Jake, and there always had been. It was all kind of backwards, but it had been from the start. They'd done what they needed to in order to get to this point, and it felt right to make the change now. "You're right."

"Of course I'm right," Jake teased, tickling Tristan's stomach and slowly working his shirt up. "That's why you married me."

"That and the choose-your-own-adventure dick game."

Jake's laugh was still the most beautiful thing Tristan had ever heard. All he wished was that he could stand between Jake and the world, so that he only ever laughed.

He'd never need to cry again if I had my way.

"Okay, husband," Jake finally murmured, his smile making dimples appear on his cheeks. "If you wanna be my husband…"

"Yes?" Tristan sat up straighter, but Jake pulled him down next to him on the bed.

"Then ride me like you mean it," Jake murmured. "Let's make the most of you getting out of work early."

Tristan growled playfully as he rolled onto Jake and nipped his ear. "Are you packing hard?"

"I might be," Jake giggled. "I've been ready for you to come home all afternoon. I was going to fuck away my sad feelings, but it turns out crafting is therapeutic, too. Now I just want to make love."

Tristan grinned. "There's an idea I can get on board with."

First, though, he had something he needed to do: kiss Jake until he couldn't remember his own name.

Their lips met in a burst of familiar warmth. However many times he kissed Jake, he was pretty sure he could never, ever get bored of it. Jake's kisses were gentle and sweet for now, like Jake was inviting him to relax. With Jake, Tristan felt safe, and comfortable, and so very at home.

Warmth crept along his skin, from the tips of his toes to

his cheeks. The spots where their bodies pressed together—along his thighs, their stomachs, his hand against the side of Jake's head—were warmest of all.

He didn't feel like he deserved this wonderful man, and his patience, and his wisdom, and his kindness... *He's made me a better man,* Tristan thought, gazing at Jake between kisses as he breathed raggedly. *And I bet he doesn't even know it.*

"You all right?" Jake whispered when Tristan took a little too long to keep kissing him, and his eyelids flickered open again.

"More than all right," Tristan answered instantly. He rubbed Jake's cheek with his thumb. "I must be the luckiest guy alive."

"Nah. That would be me," Jake teased, chucking his chin gently with two fingers before he cupped the back of Tristan's head and pulled him down for another kiss. "I think these clothes should go."

"Agreed." Tristan peeled off their clothes slowly, taking his time to admire Jake.

For once, Jake looked shy when they were naked and Tristan ran his hand carefully over his slightly swollen stomach. There was no real bump yet, but those abs had disappeared, and his pecs were fading a little, too. Instead, that certain radiance beamed from him.

"You're gorgeous," Tristan told Jake, kissing him so he had to look at him and see that he meant it. "No matter what you look like."

Jake scoffed, but he was smiling and not looking away now. "You wait until eight months into this and see."

"I can't wait," Tristan assured him, smiling. "And I'll even give you footrubs."

"Oh, I'm remembering that," Jake threatened, smirking at him.

Tristan grinned. "I hope you do." He sat up straighter, adjusting Jake's jockstrap so it sat right along his hip. He ran his hand up that hard shaft, bending it to just the right angle, and then took both of their shafts in his hand.

God, it felt good to grind against the warm silicone. So lifelike he could believe it was flesh and blood, if not for the lack of moisture at the tip. His own precum would have to suffice for them both.

He spread it gently over the heads with his palm, gasping at the extra sensation that coursed through him as soon as he added moisture.

Fuck, it felt good.

"You're so hot when you're playing with yourself," Jake informed him in a low growl. "I'll have to make you do it more." He looked so turned on right now, but he was keeping his hands off, letting Tristan stay in charge.

For now.

"I wish you could feel this," Tristan murmured.

"I can, mostly." Jake tugged his jock down and grabbed a pillow, shoving it under his hips. By the time he was done, his own smaller cock jutted out just enough that Tristan could see what he meant.

He carefully lined up his shaft with the pink, swollen head and kept his hand on top as he slid across it.

Oh, God, that felt good in a whole different way. He loved from. There was nothing like being skin on skin, and hearing Jake whimper under him made it that much more delicious. The firm pressure on a concentrated point of his own shaft made sparks race up and down sensitive skin. His cock twitched in his hand.

"Fuck, yeah," Jake approved. His hands were on Tristan's hips now, pulling him into a quick rhythm. "Come on, baby." Every little smile he gave Tristan was that much more encouragement.

As they moved, Jake kept whispering sweet nothings about how much he loved Tristan, and how he daydreamed about him when Tristan was at work.

Tristan stored that detail for later—maybe he'd sext Jake from the trailer sometime. He had the feeling that would make Jake jump his ass the minute he got through the door.

Nails bit into Tristan's hips, which grabbed Tristan's attention again in a hurry. "Yes," Jake panted, wide-eyed and twitching with pleasure. He looked close to the edge, by the way he was pushing his hips up and grinding against Tristan's cock with every thrust.

"You want me to keep going?" Tristan whispered.

Jake moaned and nodded. "Don't stop, baby. Please don't stop."

If Jake asked him to, Tristan would frot until the night ended. He leaned down to press their lips together in light kisses. "I won't stop, darling."

"I'm so close," Jake breathed against his lips, his eyes half-closed. Seeing his boyfriend—his *husband*—so close to the edge of orgasm was an utterly breathtaking sight.

"Come on, baby," Tristan murmured back, keeping his voice soft as Jake's moans grew louder. "I'm gonna ride your hard cock as soon as you come. And I'll take it slow. By the time I'm done, you'll be ready for another orgasm. I'll give you as many orgasms as you can handle tonight."

Jake gasped, his eyes wide as he grabbed the back of Tristan's head. "Yes!" he whimpered against Tristan's mouth, and his hips shuddered.

Tristan could feel his cock pulsing ever so slightly, and the subtle beauty and grace of it had him utterly hungry already.

As soon as Jake settled against the bed, Tristan pressed his lips against his cheek. "Gorgeous. God, I need you."

"Ride me." Jake grinned, his tone back to that certain authority that had Tristan wrapped around his finger. "As long as you want to." He wriggled, pulling his cock back up and settling the elastic strap on his hips. He curled his fingers around the base of his shaft to hold it steady.

Tristan nearly lunged for a condom and lube. By unspoken agreement, Jake took care of the condom while Tristan spread his legs and fingered himself, quick and dirty. He was too desperate to take long.

"I'm *so* making you do that again," Jake whispered, watching Tristan with a lazy grin on his lips. "More morning shows. And evening shows. And weekend shows."

"Baby, I'll show you whatever you want to see," Tristan moaned. His fingers already weren't enough. He pulled them out and straddled Jake. The pillow added a sharper angle, and he leaned further over Jake to keep balanced.

That meant Jake could kiss him at his leisure, and so he did, slowly pressing his lips along the sensitive skin from his ear to his collarbone, up his throat, and even his lips sometimes.

With those lips igniting the fire of need within him, Tristan ached for more. He let Jake press his cock against him, and then slowly eased himself down onto it. As he took it in, he moaned softly, his fingers curling into the bedspread and clenching tight.

Fuck, Jake felt good. Every damn time, that cock just felt like the perfect size. The initial softness gave way to a firm, long shaft that stretched him to the limit. Having Jake's cock —which was undoubtedly part of him, if not physically—so deep inside was intimate.

Whoever the hell was on top or bottom or whatever other act they were engaged in, Tristan wasn't sure anymore. He also didn't care. Making love was always different with Jake. It stood in stark contrast to the strict confines of his sex life before Jake, and it burst with vibrant love.

The way Jake caressed his cheek, the way he smiled as Tristan took him in to the base and then started thrusting... the look in his eye was unquestionably love. There was nothing of the mask Tristan saw and wore on set every day.

Anatomy didn't faze him. All his worries were gone when they made love. It was just their spirits together, and he'd never been as proud or happy to experience the joy and synchronicity of their thoughts and movements.

Whatever the hell anyone else said, two men making love was the purest, sweetest kind of energy he'd ever felt.

Ecstasy flooded Tristan's veins as his heart burst with joy. "I love you." He couldn't help but say it. It was the kind of thought that couldn't be contained.

"I love you, Tris," Jake whispered, pressing soft, open-mouthed kisses against his lips. "I love you so damn much."

Time itself seemed to blur as their bodies moved together as one. Nobody and nothing else mattered besides Jake. Their love was the only thing keeping Tristan grounded, or he might have floated off into pure bliss.

Tristan's thrusts faltered as Jake wrapped a hand around his shaft, gently stroking him in time with his thrusts. "If you keep that up..."

"Good," Jake whispered and grinned. "I'm not letting you forget about round two."

"I wouldn't dream of it," Tristan assured him, a grin flickering over his face before he nipped Jake's lower lip. "So close," he warned.

Jake stroked him faster now, and then he couldn't contain his ecstasy for one moment longer. His hips shuddered and stuttered in their rhythm. "Fuck!"

He came back to Earth what felt like an eternity later as Jake slid out of him. Jake's stomach was a lot stickier now. "Oh! You're a mess now. Oops."

Jake grinned and wriggled out of his harness setup, wrapping an arm around Jake and stroking himself with two fingers. Tristan started kissing the soft skin along Jake's shoulder and neck. The kisses made Jake gasp and squirm into him. "I like being covered in your load. Makes me feel like I'm…" he trailed off, spots of color rising to his cheeks.

"Like you're?" Tristan prompted, shivering with pleasure. Even if he'd just come, watching Jake feel so good made him hot.

"Yours."

Tristan's lips met Jake's. "You are, baby. Forever."

When Jake came, Tristan's name was on his lips, and his arm was wrapped around Tristan's back to keep their bodies pressed together so tightly that Tristan could feel every twitch and writhe of his beautiful body.

Tristan pulled Jake in close, their limbs tangling as Jake gasped for breath. He hardly knew where one of them began and the other ended, and he liked it that way.

"Forever?" Jake finally whispered, minutes after Tristan had last spoken. His gaze was wide-eyed, his cheeks so rounded from smiling that dimples appeared again.

Tristan mirrored that beautiful smile as he rubbed Jake's back. "Forever."

CHAPTER
Twenty-Seven
JAKE, TWO MONTHS LATER

"To Jake and Tristan: they do everything bass-ackwards, but they show us all what love can be."

It was all Jake could do not to tear up. For Zeph, that was a positively emotional speech.

He didn't strictly fit the tough MMA fighter stereotype, but he wasn't the most outspoken in the group. His boyfriend, River, had gushed for ages about how Jake and Tristan's budding relationship had made them all outrageously happy. Even Denver had approved. But Zeph's approval had always been quieter.

If there were ever an occasion, it was the wedding reception. Six months pregnant wasn't when most people chose to have a party to celebrate their wedding—and neither was five months after marriage.

But, exactly like Zeph had said, Jake and Tristan hadn't ever done things in the right order. They weren't about to start now.

Filming had just wrapped on Tristan's big project,

meaning he could invite a few of his castmates to come get drunk and celebrate.

Everyone Jake had met seemed like a great friend to have—all with the same kind of charisma as Tristan, but not in a fake way; they all seemed genuinely nice, and excited to meet him. They even congratulated him on the coming baby without missing a beat.

"Speech from the grooms!"

"Oh, no," Jake groaned, his cheeks flushing. They might be surrounded by all their friends, but without alcohol to help him along, he was going to remember this moment better than the rest of them.

It was a casual kind of party—no formal dress and no gifts. Woody's had agreed to rent them the bar for the after-noon, and a few of River's drag artist friends were putting on a show any moment now. In drag time, River had informed him, that could be about an hour from now. Apparently RB needed more wine to prepare.

"Oh, yes." Kyle clapped. "Speech!"

Tristan smiled and rose to his feet. "Fine, fine." He looked around at the small party, and Jake followed his gaze. Besides Tristan's coworkers—he hadn't invited his new agent, and he certainly hadn't invited Bobby after firing him last week—and their friends from Plus, Jake had invited Amanda, and a couple of friends from the queer parenting group.

Tristan had considered inviting his parents, but it was more of a friends event than family. They'd been a little distant and confused by the whole thing, but nice enough when Jake met them last month. Tristan had finally admitted to himself that he'd been holding onto hurt that he didn't need to.

Meanwhile, Jake had met Kyle and Nic's kid, Kevin,

custody of whom was shared with Kyle's best friend, Evie. All of them were the most adorable, unconventional family unit he'd ever known. It had given him hope for how his own little family could turn out.

As far as Jake was concerned, these people were his family.

"I'll go first," Jake said, and Tristan stared at him like he'd lost his mind. He patted Tristan's arm as he rose to his feet, a hand instinctively going to his stomach. If there were a few wonky seams on his clothes, nobody had commented: instead, they'd oohed and ahhed about how cool it was to see menswear that fit his body properly, unlike the baggy t-shirts he'd been wearing for the last month.

His sewing skills were getting better, but his new business was going to demand a little more improvement before he could start to sell these clothes to other people who wanted a different kind of pregnancy fashion. It was a small market, but California was one of the best places to grow this kind of business, and Tristan was behind him a hundred percent.

"I keep thinking to myself: I can't believe how we met," Jake admitted, grinning. "And I feel so damn lucky to have met my husband." Applause rang out at his use of the word, and Jake grinned. They'd been trying it out for the last few months, but it was still strange to hear, in the very best possible way. "If you'd told me a year ago that I'd be standing here, pregnant and married and starting a business and surrounded by new friends, and happier than I've ever been, I'd have laughed. But here I am. I feel..."

He was tearing up already, and he pressed his fist to his eyes. Better keep the speech short. Goddamn, he was going to be happy to get his hormones back on track.

"I've got everything I ever could have asked for, and then some. I met a man who didn't just talk about loving me. He showed me love, and he wouldn't go away until I accepted it."

Laughter rippled through the room.

"And the way you all pulled together to support me," Jake said, shaking his head. It had been Tristan's idea, but all his friends had immediately agreed to pull together a schedule so that Jake would never be unaccompanied at a doctor's appointment again.

Meanwhile, Tristan had grown ever happier and more confident from his work on the movie they'd just wrapped. He was out, and he'd found an agent who supported that, and he was throwing himself into auditions day after day. Best of all, he came home happy after auditions now, not a nervous wreck.

Tristan was shifting from foot to foot, and Jake made a mental note to swap footrubs later. His husband had spent so much time in uncomfortable shoes these last few weeks, auditioning for everything possible.

If Jake hadn't already been won over, Tristan's devotion to both Jake and their child over the last few months had melted his heart. Not only was he working hard, but he set aside whatever time he could to talk with Jake, keeping their love alive no matter how good or bad a day they'd had.

"I'm proud of Tristan, more than he'll ever know." Jake trailed off, clearing the stubborn lump in his throat. "And I'm proud to be his husband, and your friend, and... dad to this incredible little one we've got on the way. Thank you for celebrating love with us. That's all. Someone pass me the tissues."

Tristan did, patting his back and sliding an arm around his shoulders. "And for my part," he added, "I've been absolutely blessed to have you all in my life. Some of you for longer than others, but all of you are important to me—to us. And none more so than Jake." He looked over at Jake.

Oh, God. I'm gonna run out of tears by the end of today. Jake sniffled but smiled back.

"So proud of you, baby. I can't wait to see what the future has for you—for both of us. And I'm glad to call you mine."

The little bar erupted into cheers and applause, and tears rolled down Jake's cheeks as Tristan leaned in to kiss him.

It was yet another moment Jake would never forget.

He's mine, and I'm his. He kept his hand on his stomach, smiling until his cheeks hurt. *And this little one is ours, together, forever.*

"Dr. Lume!" Jake lit up with surprise and joy when his doctor walked in.

Tristan traded smiles and nods with her as she approached the bed. He hung back to let them have a moment. He hadn't told Jake that he'd gotten in touch to let her know that the birth had gone well, and they now had a new little baby: Fin.

They'd decided to raise Fin to feel as free as possible to be whoever they wanted. For now, they were going to use a mixture of pronouns to refer to Fin, and once they were talking, Jake and Tristan would see if they preferred any one in particular.

Whatever Fin wanted to be—or do, wear, say, or think, as long as it hurt nobody else—they would support them. More important was making sure Fin felt loved, always and forever.

It was a decision Tristan's parents hadn't quite been able to wrap their heads around, but they'd also never admitted that they'd driven Tristan away by trying to put restrictions on their love. Tristan had confidence they'd come around sometime, when they saw how happy Fin was going to be.

Seeing Jake light up was almost as beautiful as seeing the way he cradled their child.

Fin had Tristan's eyes and Jake's smile.

Tristan teared up every damn time he saw the two of them smiling together. In the last day, there had been a lot more tears than smiles, but after the initial panic that they would somehow break Fin before they were even home from the hospital, that first smile had been worth it all.

Jake talked with Dr. Lume for a few minutes before she bowed out of the room, leaving them in the peace and quiet and privacy of the three of them.

Their family.

"Thank you for telling her to come by," Jake murmured.

Tristan smiled and moved back to the chair beside the bed to take Jake's hand. His husband hadn't lost that wonderful glow after birth—in fact, he looked somehow even more beautiful covered in hospital blankets, with Fin lying on his chest. "Of course. I thought you might like to see her. After all, that's where all of this started."

They weren't sure if he'd be able to chestfeed Fin or not yet. Grafted nipples had a lower chance of being able to, but since his chest tissue had swollen and there had been definite leaking issues—which Tristan had assured a mortified Jake was just as beautiful as all the other changes—they were going to give it a try.

For now, skin-to-skin contact was what they all needed most of all.

Jake cast another awestruck gaze at Fin, his hand wrapped protectively around their tiny head to keep them in place as they dozed. "I can't believe we did it. That everything's okay. That we're..." Jake blinked rapidly and cleared his throat.

"That we're officially dads?" Tristan kissed the back of Jake's hand and beamed at him. "Me neither."

"I thought I was the luckiest guy in the world before they were born," Jake whispered, smiling at Tristan. "I was wrong. *Now* I am."

"No," Tristan chuckled, lacing his fingers with Jake's. "I'm pretty sure I am."

The fact that Jake had let him into his life, and let him into this whole, wonderful journey they'd already shared as well as what lay ahead...

It made Tristan feel utterly right. Maybe he'd been indecisive before, but somehow, that had gone away. His fear of rejection hadn't vanished, but it was so much quieter. So were Jake's fears, and when either of them started to act edgy, they were able to sit down and talk it out.

Through the sleepless nights ahead and the years of parenting, he would always feel like the lucky one in this relationship. And he knew Jake felt the same, which made them both try to be the best men they could for one another... and now for little Fin.

For a couple crazy young guys who'd just been trying to find themselves in L.A., they'd found so much more: each other, and a family, and hope.

"I love you," Jake whispered, his eyelids drooping. No surprise there—he'd been exhausted for the last day. He deserved to rest, with Tristan there to watch over them both.

Tristan leaned over to kiss each of his family's foreheads in turn. Jake closed his eyes and Fin shifted, but didn't wake. "I love you, too, baby," Tristan whispered. "Forever."

FREEDOM

"LIFE DOESN'T COME WITH AN INSTRUCTION MANUAL. BUT MY JUNK DOES."

Agoraphobe Jaden shouldn't have let his big brother put a ticket in a blind date raffle for him. He wasn't expecting to win. And his prize? It's an overnight trip to the Grand Canyon. This gorgeous stranger is a wilderness guide, and they couldn't be more different, but their connection is instant.

Henry's finally finished bottom surgery, and after years of staying quiet about his past, he's growing tired of hiding who he is. But the two men are rubbing off on each other: Henry helps Jaden manage his fears, and Jaden shows Henry how to be vulnerable.

Back home in Denver, both men push themselves outside their comfort zones… but freedom always comes at a price. Can they take the plunge together, and finally step into the wide-open future that's waiting?

Freedom is the fifth book in the F-Word series, which features queer found families, characters choosing their own labels, a lot of trans joy, opposites attracting, spice for days, and the happily-ever-afters we all deserve. This novel can be read as a standalone.

Rainbow Awards Winner: Best Transgender Contemporary Romance!

About the Author

E. Davies writes feel-good, low-angst romance that never fades to black when the going gets good! Born in Canada, after 16 moves and counting, Ed has finally put down roots in north London.

He emerges from his writing nest to coo over fuzzy animals, flee from cute guys, dance through the streets with his chosen family, put together fierce looks, and—most of all—befriend local flowers.

You can find all available titles at: www.edaviesbooks.com

FOLLOW E. DAVIES ONLINE:

amazon.com/author/edavies

bookbub.com/authors/e-davies

facebook.com/edaviesauthor

goodreads.com/edavies

instagram.com/edaviesauthor

x.com/edaviesauthor

Grind

Brooklyn Boys:

Electric Sunshine

Live Wire

Boiling Point

F-Word:

Flaunt

Freak

Faux

Forever

Freedom

After:

Afterburn

Afterglow

Aftermath

Shared Universes:

Shelter

Adore

Miracle

Redemption

Limelight

Barely Regal

www.ingramcontent.com/pod-product-compliance
Lightning Source LLC
Chambersburg PA
CBHW050348190726
48284CB00007BB/2199